Hot Town

and other stories

Carole

A pleasure to meet you –

Hot Town

and other stories

My sculpture forest friend

by

Janet Trull

Janet Trull

WINNIPEG

Dedicated to those of you who might recognize, somewhere in this collection of stories, an echo of your own brave myths. The ones you told me over a glass of wine or around a campfire or against your better judgment.

Contents

Hot Town

Summer moves through town like a river of slag, heavy and inevitable. Heads crack open on hot cement. Children suffocate in derelict refrigerators. People drown.

It is because of the heat, Jenny thinks, *that Warren left.* Last night she rolled over in bed and threw her arm over his broad back.

"Don't touch me," he said. He took his pillow and went out to sleep on the couch. Near dawn, Jenny awoke and listened to a thunderstorm rumbling in the distance. A sudden breeze swept past her and slammed the bedroom door. Worried that Warren would think she slammed the door in anger, Jenny creeps to the kitchen and turns on the light above the stove, not too bright, just enough light to find her way to Warren and tell him she is not mad. He hates it when she is mad.

But Warren is not on the couch. His pillow is there but Warren is gone. Jenny takes a deep breath. She showers and dresses for her job at a day camp north of the tracks where the houses are slabbed together from odds and ends of plywood and tar paper and desperation.

Most of the children at the day camp are subsidized by the Rotary Club. Most of the mothers who drop the children off are young and slovenly. They smoke. But they are not lonely. Jenny is amazed at the number of boyfriends these women go through. There is a never-ending supply of guys who don't mind a little baggage in relationships it seems. Perhaps that is why Warren is her first boyfriend since she graduated from high school six years ago. She has no baggage. No children to prove that someone found her attractive once.

Jenny met Warren at her cousin's wedding. She had expected to meet someone at college, but her small town persona hadn't transferred well to campus life. She went to bed early in her single dorm room while late night high jinks echoed up and down the halls. Now she's back home working for Parks and Rec with an air of defeat about her.

Jenny eats Cheerios and reads her horoscope. The new moon is in her sign. Good news. She will meet someone who has some advice for her. Best to listen. She puts her bowl on the floor so the cat can finish the milk. Warren hates the cat. He wants a dog.

Will Saunders parks his Impala in front of a tidy white bungalow. He walks up the gravel driveway past a police cruiser, a tent trailer up on blocks and a bicycle with bent handlebars. He lifts the latch on the chain link gate and enters the back yard. Melanie Lawson, covered in blood and badly in need of a root touch-up, is on her knees. She appears to be praying. Officer Ellis, the town's only woman cop, is keeping an eye on her, ready to cuff her if she runs. But Melanie is not likely to run. She called 911 herself.

Will tucks his notebook under his arm and blows into a pair of latex gloves. He snaps them on, opens the aluminum door and enters. The body is in the kitchen, halfway under the sink. Al

Lawson. Beer gut. Spindly legs, hairless and pale. Looks like he was fixing a leak or something when the accident happened. The screwdriver falling on him. Thirty or forty times. Will loosens his tie.

Melanie is not praying. She is watching a dragonfly trapped in a spider web. The dragonfly is fighting so hard to free itself that it is tearing its wings. Officer Ellis is touched by Melanie's concern for the struggle. She crouches beside Melanie and starts tearing the web away from the delicate wings with her pen. Melanie puts a bloody hand out to stop her.

"Don't do that," Melanie says.

The back door opens and Will gives Officer Ellis a quizzical look that has her on her feet smartly. She steps back toward the doghouse, adopting a cop stance. Arms crossed, feet planted well apart.

"Mrs. Lawson," Will says, "I need to ask you a few questions."

Melanie stands and wipes the grass off her knees. "The children will be home from day camp soon," she tells him.

"It's twelve thirty," Will says. "When do you expect them?"

"Four o'clock," she says.

"We'll have everything cleaned up by then. How old are they?"

"Eleven and thirteen," she says. "I know what you're thinking."

"What am I thinking?" Will asks, expecting the confession.

"You're thinking I'm too young to be the mother of a teenager. Everyone says so."

If you squint your eyes, Melanie still has the pretty face that got her elected prom queen in 1997. She hasn't put on weight like a lot of women her age, but the cheerleader has been sucked right out of her.

"Are you going to tell me what happened in there, Melanie?"

"He's on holidays," Melanie says.

Will is a patient man. He waits.

"The plant closes down for two weeks every August," Melanie says. "We usually go camping, but I don't know. Money's tight, I guess. My friend Sandy called and asked did I want to go to the outlet mall with her. I wasn't planning on buying anything. I was just going to look. It's air-conditioned. But Al didn't want me to go. He said, what did he take summer holidays for if his wife wasn't going to be there to enjoy them."

Will has thinning red hair, and a freckled complexion. As he writes in his notebook, the top of his head fries in the sun. He is terrified of skin cancer. His father got half his ear taken off and he doesn't want that.

"How did that make you feel?" Will asks.

Officer Ellis curses the way her black uniform attracts the sun. She spots a plastic kiddie pool by the shed, harboring layers of algae and mosquito larvae.

Jenny is supervising the kids as they have lunch under the dusty maples in Rotary Park when the cruiser pulls up. Her heart skips a beat as Reg Lumax gets out and puts on his cap and walks right toward her. It is Warren. She knows it. Dead in a car wreck. Or maybe on the job. He works construction and guys get hurt all the time. They fall into cement mixers. They chainsaw their own legs off.

"Hey, Jenny," Reg says.

"Is it Warren?"

Reg looks at her as if she's crazy, then realizes she means Warren Allen, that jerk Jenny's living with. "No, no, Jenny. It ain't Warren. I'm here for the Lawson kids." He stands real close to her and lowers his voice. "Their dad's been killed. I gotta take them into care. They can't go home."

"Oh my god. What happened?" Jenny leans in and catches a whiff of his gum. Cinnamon.

"It's a crime scene, Jenny. I can't say nothing more about it, but half the town's seen the yellow tape, so . . ."

"Murder?" Jenny asks.

"Could be," Reg says. He takes a handkerchief out of his back pocket and wipes sweat off his neck. "Anyways, I gotta take them kids to the Children's Aid. Which ones are they?"

Jenny pushes her sunglasses up on her head and scans the picnic tables. As a group, they are a scraggly bunch, sharing their sandwiches with seagulls from the dump. Jenny thought she liked kids until she started working with poor kids. They make her feel hopeless. She can't seem to motivate them. "What do you expect," Warren tells her when she worries about their lethargy and lack of prospects. "You can't polish turds," he says. Even so, Brittney Lawson stands out among them as singularly unloved, wearing a stretched-out bathing suit that looks like a hand-me-down from a fatter cousin.

"That's Brittney at the end of the bench."

"Blonde? Bad posture?"

"Yep. That's her."

"Where's the boy?"

"Over there, under the slide. He's the oldest kid at camp."

"Okie dokie then," Reg says, hoisting up his trousers by the waistband. "You and Warren coming to the arena Saturday for the Fish Fry?"

"Don't know yet," Jenny says. She is a little bit disappointed that the crisis does not involve Warren. His death would have released her from her responsibilities. Now she has to organize the kids for afternoon activities. It is too hot for soccer. Maybe she'll take them down to the creek and look for frogs.

Officer Ellis has dumped out the stagnant water and started filling the plastic pool with the hose. She runs cool water over her wrists and feels some relief.

"I could use a drink," Will says. "Do you want a drink, Melanie? Are you thirsty?"

"Yes," she says in a soft baby voice. "There's lemonade in the fridge."

"Officer," Will says. "Can you grab the pitcher of lemonade out of the fridge and maybe a couple glasses?"

Officer Ellis sets the hose down in the pool. Except for a little eddy of swirling grass around the nozzle, it is hard to tell the water is running. It's likely against procedure, disturbing a crime scene to get a drink, but since the Coroner asked she figures it must be all right. Besides. It's hot as hell and she wants a drink too.

"The suspect wants a drink," she announces to the detectives in the kitchen. They don't say a word because she has not really asked permission so she just opens the fridge and grabs the lemonade. In the cupboard, the one over the stove, she finds a stack of plastic glasses. She reaches over a pot that is crusted with Zoodles and crawling with flies. A dog is barking down in the basement.

"Thanks," she says on her way out the door.

"Uh-huh," the young detective says. Officer Ellis suspects that the Pepsi he has in his hand is from the case in the victim's fridge.

Not that Al would've had a problem with that. Al had it in him to be an asshole, but he wasn't cheap. She knew that for a fact.

Officer Ellis opens the back door with her hip and sets the lemonade down on a little plastic table. Then she arranges some chairs around the pool. She kicks off her black oxfords, balls up her sweaty black socks, rolls up her pants. She looks over at Will and with a tilt of her head invites him over. *Strange or not*, Will thinks, *the officer has a brain in her head*. He helps Melanie get settled into a chair. She slips her calloused feet into the water.

"Oh. That feels good," she says. She accepts a cup of lemonade, gulps it down and asks for more, then carefully tucks the cup under her chair.

"Now, Melanie," Will says. "What do you remember after Al asked you to hand him the screwdriver?"

"That was when the accident took place," Melanie says. She lifts her right foot out of the water, lays it across her left knee and starts picking dirt out from underneath the nail of her big toe.

The back door opens and the older detective summons Will. Thunder rolls, long and low in the distance. Melanie takes her feet out of the pool. Officer Ellis grabs the hose and sprays some water in the direction of the withered begonias over by the fence. She blasts the spider web. The dragonfly hovers briefly and balances on a leaf before it flies off. Melanie watches, clearly annoyed. She glares at the officer.

"You from out of town?" Melanie asks.

"Nope. I sat behind you in grade six. Mr. Disher's class. I was at your sweet sixteen birthday party, too."

Melanie looks the officer up and down, challenging the disclosures with a long exhausting pause. Crawling back through the shadowy culvert that is her memory, she finds no record of this woman as a girl. "You want a dog?" she asks.

Jenny bikes home the long way, past the Lawson house. An SPCA worker is leading a Rottweiler to the truck.

"You want a dog?" Reg asks her as she pulls up alongside his cruiser.

Jenny leans forward on her handlebars and looks at her reflection in Reg's sunglasses. "I don't like dogs," she says.

"Me neither," says Reg. "Particularly I don't like that dog. He hampered the investigation. Licked most of the blood up before Homicide arrived."

Jenny watches as the dog is muzzled and locked inside the truck. "How are the kids?" she asks.

"They're okay. They're at a foster home."

"You done work soon?" Jenny asks.

"Yep. My shift ends at five."

"Want to go for a drink later?"

Reg pauses and looks carefully at Jenny to determine whether she is joking around or serious. He has trouble with social cues sometimes. "I thought you were with Warren," he says.

"Not anymore," Jenny says.

"Then sure," Reg says.

"Meet you at Pee Wee's at seven," Jenny tells him and then cycles off. Reg watches her muscular glutes working rhythmically atop the padded bicycle seat. He notices that she doesn't stop at the stop sign. And she isn't wearing a helmet.

Jenny pushes the door to her apartment open. Warren is sitting on the couch in his boxers. His hair is wet and slicked back from a recent shower. The fan is two feet away, aimed right at him. He has a beer in one hand and the clicker in the other. Some doctor on a talk show is answering questions about bowel movements.

"Hey," he says. "You hear about the murder?"

Jenny takes a good look at him, half-nude and hairy on her white couch. "The Lawson kids go to my day camp," she says. "Reg came and picked them up."

"Reg come on to you?"

"Why would he?"

"He likes you."

"How would you know that?"

Warren doesn't answer. Instead he holds out the empty beer bottle for her. She takes it to the kitchen and gets him a cold one. This is not the day to tell him to get his own damn beer.

"Did the kids cry?"

"What?"

"The Lawson kids. Did they cry when Reg told them about their dad?"

"He didn't tell them. He just told them they were going for a ride in the cruiser."

"And they got in? They didn't ask why?"

"They're not stupid," Jenny says. "They've been waiting for something bad to happen for a long time."

Days of Our Lives

Since Gordon died I get tired sometimes. Weary. I must have closed my eyes, just for a second.

Brad called and asked me if I could babysit Michael for the afternoon, and well, I was just about to lie down. But I hate to say no to Brad. My daughter-in-law, she has never liked me and when the little guy was born she was always looking over my shoulder whenever I held him. My own grandson. She was quick to criticize the way I put his diaper on, or fed him non-organic food.

Oh for heaven's sake, Brad ate canned spaghetti and Alphabets and he's never been sick a day in his life. She's a project, that woman, and Brad has his hands full. She's some kind of executive at a financial institution. Wealth management, they call it now. And she takes every chance she's got to tell everyone that she's the main breadwinner in her family. That's why Brad stayed home after Michael was born, so she didn't lose a chance to get promoted. Well, Brad was never very ambitious. He'd rather sail or ski. But he's back working in real estate and that's a competitive field. So when he gets a call to show some property, he calls me.

I know his wife wanted Brad to put the little guy in daycare, but fourteen months is pretty young for that, not old enough to defend himself or tell what went on. I offered to help out, but it is tiring. You cannot turn around to plug the kettle in with a fourteen month old baby in the house for fear he will fall down the stairs or stick something in his mouth.

The day it happened, I went for a walk in the morning with the seniors group. We did the botanical garden loop and by the time we climbed up through the lilac dell, I was sweating with the heat. It got up to thirty degrees, apparently, but it wasn't real humid like some days are. No smog, just nice clear skies with some puffy bits of cloud. There'd be rain before midnight, but you'd never guess it by the weather at midday.

I unlocked the door, hung my purse on the newel post, and the phone rang. It was Brad. "I'm on my way," I told him. "Be there in twenty minutes." I put my purse back on my shoulder, dug for my keys, and got back in the car. It was still cool from the A/C.

Brad looked nice in a shirt and tie. He'd shaved that scruffy beard off, too. It was good to see him taking care of his appearance again. He scooped Michael up and passed him to me with the diaper bag and said, "Thanks, Mom, I owe you. I'll come get him around five?"

"Five," I said. "That's fine."

I have my own car seat for the baby. I buckled the little guy in. Such a good little man, but wiggly, and I'm not as strong as I once was. He's hefty. Twenty-five pounds. We took Governor's Road, which was a mistake because lunch hour was finishing up at the school and we had to wait for a light and a crossing guard and a school bus turning, so by the time we got to my turn-off, the little guy had nodded off. I was not happy about that. I was hoping I could put him down and he'd sleep while I put my feet up. But I knew he would never go down again. Even if he napped for five minutes, even two minutes, that would be it for sleeping. He'd be tearing around until Brad came at five. It was going to be a long afternoon.

I expected Michael to wake up when I opened the garage door, but no, he did not stir. *He must be tired*, I thought. If he wasn't so heavy, I might have even tried to carry him in and put him in the little playpen I keep in the guest bedroom. Instead, I decided to let him sleep for a few more minutes while I made a sandwich. I was hungry from all that exercise in the morning and I'd been looking forward to a toasted tomato. The tomatoes I'd bought at the farmers market on Saturday were the best I'd had in a long time. My hips were aching badly from the morning's hike and I swallowed a couple of Tylenol 3's while I waited for the toast to pop. That sandwich with extra mayonnaise? Delicious. I enjoyed that sandwich. Every bite.

I sat on the couch and turned on my show, *General Hospital*, which I've been following since Brad was breastfeeding. I remember thinking that I'd wait until the first commercial and then I'd get up and get Michael. Maybe he'd play quietly with the basket of cars I kept for him under the coffee table.

But the next thing I remember is the music to *The Young and the Restless*. I was feeling kind of dozy and I watched for a minute or so, wondering what Victor was doing on the wrong show. Then I felt a punch in the stomach. Just exactly like that, as if somebody had slugged me in the gut and took the wind out of me. And I jumped off the couch and ran to the garage and *please god please god please god*, opened it. *Please god please god,* and the garage was hot, hot, hot. And I yanked open the door, *please god please god please . . .* and he was slick with sweat, slumped in the seat. Unnatural looking. I knew right away that he was gone. And that was terrible. But it was my fault. And that made it unbearable. I tried to lift him, but he was dead weight, literally, and I was weak with despair and all I wanted was to crawl in there with him and die. I had to get him inside. Cool him down, then maybe I wouldn't be blamed. Maybe, they would think crib death or something. Something terrible, but not as terrible as a neglectful grandmother who fell asleep in front of a soap opera. Nothing in the world could be as bad as that.

I somehow managed to hoist him out of the seat and lay him on the kitchen table and *please god please god please god* I prayed that the cool air would somehow revive him. A miracle, is that too much to ask? I gave him mouth to mouth and glanced at the clock and saw it was 4:45 and Brad would be coming soon to pick him up and how was I going to fix this?

Only then did I think to call 911.

When Brad pulled up, there was an ambulance and a police cruiser in front of my townhouse and all the neighbours were out gawking, and I was trying to explain to a very young officer how a grandma could leave a little baby in a car on a hot day. How? I don't know. *It was an accident.*

I just closed my eyes for a second.

Yellow Camaro

It is 1972. I am seventeen. For the rest of my life, I will never be as thin, or as beautiful as I am this day in February, but neither will I be as self-loathing. I hate my skin. Acne is all I see when I look at myself in the mirror. I hate my teeth. I hate the retainer that is straightening them. I hate my height. The boy I like is shorter than me by two full inches. Platform shoes are the newest style in footwear, and my true love has a pair. His name is Pat. It is coming up to Valentine's Day and I am half expecting Pat to ask me to go to dinner someplace special where we will dress up. Shakespeare's Steak House is nice, where the waiters light your cigarettes with elegant gold lighters. I am hoping Pat will present me with a promise ring. Star sapphires are popular. But, unless he is waiting to surprise me, the possibility is getting more and more remote. I am bracing myself for disappointment. Years from now, I will meet Pat and his husband at an upscale bakery buying sourdough bread. But this day there is no reassurance for the indifference he offers.

It is dreary as I leave the house with last night's homework, two textbooks balanced on a clipboard. This is how we carry our schoolbooks in the days before backpacks. We don't expect a boy to carry our books, as was common in the fifties and sixties. Those days are over. We carry our own books and open our own doors. We won the right, through sit-ins, to wear pants to school. We think we are rebels. We think we are feminists. But our convictions are easily shaken and our victories lead to unisex everything. Hair, jeans, sweatshirts. Soon gender is a moot point. Everyone is equally sloppy and miserable and unemployable.

I am wearing the tweed maxi coat that I made in home-ec along with a long crocheted scarf. My friend Sasha and I have sewing machines and we make most of our own clothes. Even our jeans. We buy the denim from the ancient, skeletal Mr. Burnside who owns the Dry Goods store on the corner of Queen and Main. We sew our jeans tight, tight, tight, down to the knees where they flare to raggedy hems that drag along slushy sidewalks. We alter the Butterick patterns so that the jeans ride low on our hips with big fat belt loops for our big fat belts.

Sasha is waiting for me at the corner. Even bundled in her navy double-breasted maxi coat (yes, she made it in home-ec) she is bent and angular like a jackknife with all the blades out. She is having her first cigarette of the day and she passes it over as she falls into step alongside me. I take a drag, feel the first dizzy buzz of nicotine, and pass it back to her.

"Did Pat call?"

"No."

"Maybe he's waiting to surprise you."

"I don't think so. I'm not holding my breath."

Sasha loves Mike, a high school dropout who drives a yellow Camaro. He pumps gas at the Esso station out on the highway.

"Did you see Mike last night?"

"Ummhmm."

"Yes?"

"Yeah."

"Well?"

"We went to the Grandview."

"The motel? The no-tell motel?"

"Yeah."

This is unexpected. We have seen lots of girls get themselves in trouble. Trudy was the first, in grade nine. Then there was Sharon and Judith in grade ten. We observe the humiliation. The loss of reputation. We are smarter than those girls. But now that we are seventeen, the boys we like are more persistent. They murmur mean words when we bat their hands away from our bra straps or the buttons we have sewn on our jeans. "C'mon," they say. "Don't be a CT." CT is short for cock-teaser and no one wants to be that. Once that rubbery appendage is released, it is difficult to get it back where it belongs. The urgency is compelling. Disturbing. Irresistible. "Of course I respect you," the boys say.

But really? The respectable girls are babysitting on Friday nights or bowling with the Baptist Youth, not driving around with six packs of beer and eventually ending up on the Bird Road. The Bird Road is where the boys park their cars. "Trust me. I would never hurt you," they say as they wrestle you into the back seat. Or if they have reclining seats, they manoeuver themselves over to your side to take the gearshift out of play.

"Did you give in?"

"Yep."

"Tell me."

"We got a room with two double beds. Jack and Rosie were on the other bed."

It takes me a while to digest this. To picture it. I have been in motel rooms before with my parents and brothers. Two double beds and a TV and a bathroom. A rollaway for the little brother. And Magic Fingers. For a quarter you can enjoy a massage. The mattress will vibrate for fifteen minutes and leave you buzzing for an hour.

"We shared a twenty-sixer of rye and then we turned off the lights and made out."

"Wait. Rosie? Roseanne Mitchell? She's huge! She's due any day now!"

"At least she can't get pregnant."

"What about you? Did you . . . did you use a . . . "

"Condom? Of course!"

"Did it hurt?"

"Of course."

"Did it feel . . . how did it . . . do you want to do it again?"

"It's all right. It's more for him. His, you know. Pleasure."

That is not how we have dreamed about losing our virginity. The Grandview is not even a nice motel. It has broken windows. No travellers stay there overnight. It rents by the hour.

"Do you think I'm a slut?"

"What? No! Of course not. But I don't think Mike is good enough for you. You're way too smart for him."

At school, we duck into the smoking area, a courtyard out of the wind behind the old gym. There are bullet holes in the far wall. This is where the gun club used to practice before it was cancelled as an extra curricular activity. I dig around in my fringed suede purse to find the blue and white package with my cigarettes. Sasha reaches out with a match, exposing a thin bruised wrist.

"Did he do that? Mike?"

"He can't help it. He's strong."

Mike is rough. A former football player, once muscular, now simply fat. His dad is a Class A Mechanic. A good one. Everybody takes their cars to him. But Mike is not like his dad. He is lazy. And he is not somebody you would trust with your car. You just wouldn't. So Mike pumps gas and that is all.

Snow is falling. Not the pretty, fat flakes. This stuff is more like sleet, mean-spirited and oppressive. We step on our smoldering butts and go inside, heading for our lockers at the far end of the tech wing. We picked these lockers on purpose to be close to the tech boys who take shop and auto mechanics. These boys can change the oil in their own cars. They build stuff and weld metal and they have more testosterone than the boys in our arts and science classes. We hang up our coats and head to math. Then French. Then chemistry.

At lunch, Sasha wants to stand out front in case Mike drives by in his Camaro. We share a bag of chips and a carton of chocolate milk before the yellow car comes crawling along the bus lane. Mike has his friend Jack with him, a forklift driver and champion bull-shitter who never shuts up. We hop in and they drive us around, trying to convince us to take the afternoon off. The drinking age has just been dropped to eighteen and they know a bar out in Selkirk that doesn't ask for ID. We could get in, no problem. A tray of draft is two bucks. That's ten beer. That's like twenty cents a beer. "The owner's name is Sudsy," says Jack. "He knows us."

I have a history test in the afternoon, so I get them to drop me off. But Sasha is in love. She is going to Selkirk with them. She is ready to have a good time. Sasha is super smart. Smarter than me. Her parents came over from Yugoslavia. It was bad there. They speak in broken English and work the graveyard shift in the pickle factory. They yell a lot in Slovak, or whatever the hell language it is. When I go to her place, we hurry up to Sasha's room with Eastern European accusations chasing us. We paint our nails and open the window to flick our cigarette ashes carelessly, brazenly into the garden below. They drift down past the kitchen window where Sasha's mother is always chopping or scrubbing, a squat, angry, sweaty woman who has endured untold hardships and endeared herself to no one.

The Camaro stops at the side door behind the gym. Before I get out, I hand Sasha a two-dollar bill and a dime.

"The first round is on me," I tell her.

The dime is for the pay phone, in case she needs it. It's our joke. Sasha laughed at my mother when we were on the way to the Halloween Dance last year with a couple of choirboys.

"Have you got a dime in your purse?" my mother asked. "A girl should always carry a dime in case she gets stranded."

Sasha never has cash on her. I do. I work at my father's store on Saturdays. The minimum wage has gone up to $1.20 an hour, so I always have a bit of cash in my wallet. Sasha works summers at the cannery, but she socks most of it away for college. She wants to be a dental assistant. She is smart enough to be a dentist, but she wants to get married and have kids. She wants a nice house with a pool. She wants a Mustang in the driveway. These are the things we talk about while we paint our nails. We are shy about our dreams, like orphans who

19

don't dare hope for real parents. That is why I am burdened with the knowledge that Sasha's dreams are dead. They must be dead. We know the kind of husband that will mow the lawn and take our future children to hockey practice at six in the morning, and Mike is not one of them. Our egos are not big enough to consider doctors or lawyers, but we might marry a bank manager or a high school teacher. We might get someone with benefits and clean fingernails.

I walk home alone. I don't really expect to see the yellow Camaro so my heart jumps a little when it pulls into a driveway right in front of me, nearly running over my foot. Jack rolls down his window.

"Where's your friend?"

"What do you mean?"

"She changed her mind about coming with us to Selkirk."

"Sasha? Where is she?"

"That's what we want to know. We dropped her off at school just after we dropped you off. She said she better should write that history test after all."

Sasha is not in my history class. She doesn't even take history. She is taking geography this term. My heart pounds fast and hard in my chest. Mike leans over and looks at me. I cannot see his eyes behind the mirrored aviators. He points at me in a vaguely threatening way.

"You better get home, little girl."

There is no answer at Sasha's house until her little sister picks up the phone at four thirty.

"Is Sasha there?"

"No, not yet. The door was locked when I got home."

"Tell her to call me when she gets in."

"Okay."

Sasha does not show up. When her parents get home from the afternoon shift at midnight, they call the police who tell them to wait twenty-four hours. Cops can't waste their time on troubled teenagers. Immigrant's kids. Kids of factory workers.

Sasha's dad stomps the two blocks to the police station and starts screaming at them in his heavy accent. They take down Sasha's description and send a cruiser to check out the usual flophouses in Slab Town, the decrepit neighbourhood down by the river that has been notorious for bootlegging for a hundred years and now is becoming notorious for LSD and pot and orgies.

Mike and Jack stick with their story about dropping Sasha off at school. I say nothing. Nothing about the Grandview Motel or the bruise or the lunchtime car ride or the veiled threat after school. I do not confide in our friends who are gossipy and quick to blame bad girls for their own undoing. I walk home past the Catholic Church, Sasha's church. I am tempted to go in and seek out the priest. Tell him. Unburden myself. I am tempted to stop in at Sasha's house. It looks forlorn as February turns to March. The tar paper siding is designed to look like bricks, but it doesn't fool anyone. March melts away into April and still the skies are greenish grey. Sasha is not located until Easter weekend when a farmer notices a dozen turkey vultures circling his cornfield.

The day they found Sasha I sat by the river and watched it rush over the dam. Her coat was found two kilometers away from her body, the buttons scattered along the ditch of the Bird Road. Good quality brass buttons that her mom paid extra for. They wouldn't have come off easily. Sasha used heavy-duty thread for buttons. She anchored them with a smaller button on the back. My dime was still in her pocket.

No one was ever charged.

I walk to school with Martha now. She lives in a big stone house on Broad Street. Her dad is the judge. Martha is applying to McGill and U of T. She wants to study music and art history. She is getting out of this town and never coming back. It sounds like a good idea to me.

The guidance counselor doesn't seem surprised when I tell him that I want to apply to university. "Take anything except women's studies or phys-ed," he recommends. "That's where all the lesbians are." Lesbians sound exotic and refreshing. There are none in my town. I am hopeless at team sports so I sign up for women's studies.

After the Wedding

A woman (Julia) sits on the side of a bed with a sheet wrapped around her. She picks up her purse from the floor and finds her brush. She crosses the room to the dresser and brushes her hair in front of the mirror. She wrinkles her nose at a smell, and notices a pair of men's shoes on top of the dresser. She moves them to the floor and returns to sit on the side of the bed. She digs around for Chapstick in her purse and is applying it to her lips when a man enters.

A man (Brad) stares at the woman sitting on his bed, then he stares at the shoes.

Julia: They were on top of the dresser.
Brad: I know. They're my dad's shoes.
Julia looks at the shoes as if she needs a bit more information.
Brad: He died.
Julia: Sorry. For your loss. Was it . . . recent?
Brad: Yes.
Julia looks at the shoes again and raises her eyebrows.

Brad: When I went to the funeral home they gave me his shoes. You know. They said they don't usually put a guy's shoes on him in the coffin. So I brought them home and put them there.

Julia: They wouldn't have said *coffin*.

Brad: What? Sure they would. Did.

Julia: Coffin is like a pioneer word. Jesse James would have been laid to rest in a coffin.

Brad: What would you call it?

Julia: Casket. It's a casket.

Brad: Hmmm. Don't think so. Pretty sure he said coffin. But, come to think of it. The funeral director did look like a pioneer. Old dude with a bolo tie.

Brad picks up the shoes and puts them back on the dresser.

Julia: They smell. That's why I put them on the floor when I was brushing my hair. Sorry. I didn't mean to offend you. Or your dad.

Brad: That's okay. You didn't know. You want some breakfast?

Julia: No. Thanks. I have to work today.

Brad: It's Sunday.

Julia: I work in an art gallery two Sundays a month.

Brad: Want coffee?

Julia: No. I have a little routine at the gallery. Lights, cash register, coffee. I'm the kind of person that likes a routine. Once I get one in place, it's best if I don't mess with it.

Brad: You like things orderly.

Julia: Yep. There's enough chaos in the world.

Brad: Like shoes sitting in places where they don't belong.

Julia: I admit I prefer shoes on the floor. Your dad must have meant a lot to you.

Brad: He was a barber. Him and his brother had a shop called the Clipper Ship.

Julia: That's clever. (*Pause*) There aren't many real barber-shops anymore.

Brad: I know. They made a good living with it. The waiting chairs were always full of retired guys. If a working guy came in they'd be like, go ahead, son, we're in no hurry. Half the time the old boys didn't need a haircut at all, just wanted to talk about fishing lures and hunting.

Julia: It's sad. The disappearing landscape of male culture.

Brad has no response to that. It sounds like bullshit to him. He scratches himself. Julia fiddles nervously with a chain around her neck.

Julia: So did he wear those shoes in the shop?

Brad: Sure. They probably have remnants of human hair on the soles.

Julia: That's a lot of DNA.

Brad: (*Gives her a look as if she might be a whack job*) My dad was cheap. Thrifty. He never bought a new pair of shoes until the old pair was worn right out. Then he'd take the shoes across the street to Toots Overholt and get them re-soled.

Julia: Toots?

Brad: Toots was the shoe repairman. They had a deal. Free haircuts for free soles.

Julia: (*Laughs*) Sounds like your dad got the better part of that deal. (*Brad looks confused.*) You know. It must be nice to get a new soul. (*Brad tilts his head.*) Never mind.

Brad: I get it. Like, save your soul. The re-soling business is dead. You can buy new shoes for what Toots charged for those rubber soles. But I loved the smell of his shop. The leather, I guess.

Julia: Lost soles. A failed civilization is humanity.

Brad: Yep. Old Toots saved a lot of shoes from ending up in the landfill.

Awkward pause. Julia roots around in her purse and finds some Tic Tacs.

Julia: Want one?

Brad: Sure.

Julia: So, your dad. His funeral was here in town?

Brad: Ya. Over three hundred people came to his funeral. You woulda thought their own dads had died. The end of an era, they said. He never had a cash box. He just pocketed the money and moved the peg one spot on his cribbage board for each haircut.

Julia: Did he play cribbage, or just use the board to keep track of his cuts?

Brad: They had two boards. A playing board and a tracking board. My dad and Uncle Pete played whenever it was slow.

Julia: Do you play?

Brad: Used to. You?

Julia: I haven't played in a long time. I never got the hang of counting. Fifteen two. Fifteen four. (*She looks around and sees her underwear on the floor. Stretches her leg out and grabs them with her toes, trying to look casual.*) Is your uncle still alive?

Brad: No. Uncle Pete went first. The shop is for sale, but nobody wants it.

Julia: Can you cut hair?

Brad: I can, but I'm not a confident barber. You have to be able to grab a guy's head and turn it this way. That way. Push it down to trim the neckline. And also? You have to talk the whole time about hockey or what's going on at town hall. It's a real skill to make a guy forget you've got sharp scissors and razors near his ears and his eyes.

Julia: His eyes?

Brad: Oh ya. Old guys need their eyebrows trimmed. And their nose hairs and their ear hairs. All that stuff grows way faster than the hair on their heads.

Julia: You could hire a barber. You know. Manage the shop and pay a barber.

Brad: No money in it. Besides, I got enough going on.

Julia: What do you do?

Brad: Rec Director. I run the arena and the playing fields. And the public washrooms in the park. My favourite part of the job.

Julia: *(Laughs)* My dad had a septic pumping business.

Brad: He drove the honey wagon?

Julia: Yes. Actually he *owned* the honey wagon. He had a cartoon of a bumblebee painted on the side of his truck, holding his nose with a caption that said, *P .U. That ain't honey*!

Brad: So you must've grown up in a rural area.

Julia: Wilberforce.

Brad: Yep. Rural. He still alive?

Julia: Depends how you define alive. He sits in a dark room and watches *Storage Wars* all day.

Brad: Does he still have his honey wagon shoes?

Julia: *(Laughs)* I doubt it. If he did, he wouldn't be putting them on his dresser. Actually, he was meticulous about his work stuff. Kept everything pristine. His tools are still his pride and joy. If you borrow something from his work-bench, you better get it back in the right place, or there'll be hell to pay.

Brad: What's his favourite screwdriver?

Julia: Robertson. Why?

Brad: You can tell a lot about a guy by the kind of screwdriver he prefers. Robertsons are for smart guys who work fast. You can tighten a screw with one hand. Drink a beer with the other. Good Canadian product.

Julia: *(Looks at him as if he just said something surprisingly really smart. As if a curtain was pulled aside and she can see intelligence behind the idiot.)* Right, eh? A slot head is only good for lightweight jobs, like screwing a light switch in place. And a Phillips? How many times have you stripped a screw with a damn Phillips? Useless!

Brad: Can I drive you to work?

Julia: I drove us here last night, remember? Your car is still at the Legion.

Brad: Thanks for that. I shouldn't have started drinking scotch.

Julia: Not an issue. You want me to drop you at your car on my way to work?

Brad: No. That's okay. I'll walk over later. Get some fresh air.

Julia: So, are you Scott's friend?

Brad: No. Friend of the bride. Danielle is my ex-wife.

Julia: The bride is your ex-wife? You didn't mention that last night. When did she leave?

Brad: About midnight.

Julia: I mean when did she leave *you*?

Brad: She didn't. I left.

Julia: When?

Brad: Three years ago. She had an affair with a dude at her school.

Julia: Not Scott?

Brad: No. Some married dude. The principal, actually.

Julia: Did you go to counseling?

Brad: No. I have a code about marriage. Zero tolerance for sleeping around.

Julia: Did you learn that in the barbershop?

Brad: Maybe. Those old boys didn't respect guys who weren't in charge of their women. *Pussy-whipped* it was called. In the old days. Not now. You dare not say that nowadays. You're not married, are you?

Julia: No.

Brad: Were you? Ever?

Julia: No. Engaged once. To Scott.

Brad: The groom? You didn't mention that last night.

Julia: We were eighteen. He gave me a tiny little diamond. Said it was a pre-engagement ring. So, maybe we weren't engaged really. Just engaged to be engaged.

Brad: What happened?

Julia: I dumped him. He was crazy.

Brad: Like, how crazy?

Julia: Like jealous and controlling and angry all the time. Once we were driving along Queen Street and a bunch of high school boys were on the sidewalk. Just walking along. And I turned my head to look at them and he flipped out.

Brad: Hit you?

Julia: No. He shoved me the odd time, but he never hit me. He was unpredictable. You couldn't guess what would set him off. That day, he slammed on the brakes and pulled over and screamed at me to get out. If you like other guys so much, he says, go and be with them. He was yelling loud enough so people were turning to look.

Brad: Did you get out?

Julia: Hell yes. I started walking home and he followed me real slow in his car screaming at me to get back in.

Brad: And yet, you're still friends.

Julia: Sort of. I'm best friends with his sister, which is how I got the invitation. He's not an axe murderer or anything, but your ex-wife has got herself a real project.

Brad: You remind me of her.

Julia: Seriously?

Brad: Ya. Organized. The towels were always hanging perfect in the bathroom. Couldn't even use them to wipe my mouth in case I got toothpaste on them, so I had to keep a towel hidden under the sink that I was allowed to get dirty.

Julia: You think I'm like that because I put your dad's shoes on the floor?

Brad: Well, it could be an indicator.

Julia: Of what?

Brad: Of OCD. Obsessive…

Julia: I know what OCD is. And, believe me. I haven't got it. OCD people have these repetitive behaviours that interfere with their ability to get on with their day. They wash their hands until they bleed. I'm not OCD, I'm just happier when I have the details of my life sorted out.

Brad: So, do you ever re-stack the dishwasher after somebody else loads it?

Julia: Sure. If they do it wrong. Lots of people have no idea how to stack a dishwasher.

Brad: And the pots?

Julia: Always by hand.

Brad: That's OCD.

Julia: No. It's just smart. If you put the pots on the bottom shelf, nothing on the top gets clean. And if you put the pots on the top shelf, they stop the water spinner from turning properly.

Brad: And nothing gets clean.

Julia: Right.

Brad: How old are you?

Julia: 48. You?

Brad: 45. Kids?

Julia: No. You?

Brad: No. You want kids?

Julia: I'm 48. I'm peri-menopausal.

Brad: What's that?

Julia: It means if I wanted kids at one time, I don't anymore. That dream is dead.

Julia stands up, grabs her clothes, and walks to the bathroom. Brad throws his dad's shoes in the closet, and goes to the kitchen to start the coffee. When Julia comes out, she is dressed in the outfit she wore to the wedding. But her hair is pulled up in a knot on top of her head.

Brad: You're pretty hot for a woman who's almost fifty.

Julia: Nice backhanded compliment.

Brad: Just honesty. It's part of my code.

Julia: And part of your curse.

Brad: Want to meet for dinner on Tuesday?

Julia: Tuesday's good.

Brad: You cook?

Julia: Not much. You?

Brad: Not much. O'Grady's, then? Tuesday is Trivia Night at O'Grady's.

Julia: Okay. Seven?

Brad: Seven, it is. I'm always right on time. It's part of my code.

Julia grabs her purse and walks out the door without saying goodbye.

Brad leans against the counter, arms crossed. He picks up his phone.

Brad: Dad? Hey . . . yeah, had a great time. I met somebody. Got a date for Tuesday night . . . thanks for lending me your suit. I'll bring it by tonight . . . Mom cooking roast beef? Yeah. Yeah, sure! I won't forget your shoes.

Embracing Decay

"Get me something from the woods," Ryan says.

Andrea nods, pulling the chain on the light so he can sleep. It is her fault he has cancer. She didn't breastfeed him long enough. And she was a clean freak when he was little, exposing him to all kinds of toxic chemicals. Windex and weed killer.

Once the hospital doors close behind her it is November, frost-crisped and grey. She finds the trail that takes her down through the woods to a stream. In August she brought Ryan leaves and he identified every one. In September she brought acorns and berries and sumac fruit. In October, cattails and asters. Today she finds a delicate chain of seed pods strung across bare bushes like garland. Ryan will know what they are.

Andrea has learned to love the chaos of the forest. Vines corkscrew around branches, pulling and strangling; a messy texture of generational creation and destruction. Nobody disinfects or tidies up. Trees fall and die and decompose among the skunk cabbage and soon, new little seedlings force their way toward sunlight.

When she returns to the hospital, Ryan's room is pungent with the smell of rot.

33

"Wild cucumber," Ryan says. "Echinocystis lobata."

Andrea arranges it along the shelf with some milkweed and thistles. Ryan slips away while her back is turned.

Cole is caught off-guard by the night wind, drawing him into the same old vortex of longing and adrenaline that leads, invariably, to bad luck. He is violating two of the conditions of his parole and no doubt he will be mad at himself tomorrow. But right now, with the leaves swirling around him and the laughter of Gordie and Ox egging him on, he doesn't care. The vodka and the pills are working their magic. He is brave and invincible as his skateboard sings along the wall of the escarpment. Looking up at the full moon, golden and benevolent, Cole is riding through the universe like a hero.

So, when his front wheel catches a crack in the cement and kicks him over the cliff, he feels let down, once again, by the unreliable quality of his own super powers. Just before he passes out, he is humiliated by the cackling laughter of his friends. When he comes to, the paramedics are reassuring him that he's going to be fine.

"We'll call your parents."

Cole knows that he looks about sixteen, but he is twenty-one. He has been living on his own since his mother moved back to Halifax.

"Next of kin, then? Who do you want us to call?"

The only person that Cole can think of is Randy, his parole officer. Randy won't be in the office until 8:30 in the morning. There will be no one to meet him at the hospital. Ox and Gordie took off, leaving him for dead. Lydia, his roommate, has a new boyfriend named Jason, so Cole's been making himself scarce. Lydia's pregnant and she wants a dad for her kid. For some messed up reason, she thinks Jason might fit the bill. Jason is a douche. A stupid douche. He hasn't done the math. Lydia is seven months pregnant and she has only known Jason for, like, twelve weeks. Cole's chest buzzes with worry until the morphine kicks in. When Randy shows up at ten-thirty the next morning, he is still on a gurney in the hallway.

"What the hell did you do to yourself, now?" Randy says.

"I'm starving. Any chance you can smuggle some food in here?"

"Sure. There's a Subway across the street. What kind you want?"

"Meatball. And could you see if you can find out what happened to my backpack? I can't remember if I had it in the ambulance."

"Leave it to me," Randy says.

Randy is reliable. For Cole, that's the best characteristic to have. Reliability. He tries to be a reliable person himself. If he says he's going to do something, most of the time he does it. Randy wants him to take a college course so he can get his shit together, but there's this essay he has to write about his goals and he can't get past the first couple of sentences.

Cole is feeling optimistic when the orthopedic surgeon sends him for x-rays. He likes the hospital and he hopes he can stay. Nothing good has happened to him in a while. If he gets admitted, he'll have three square meals a day and sleeping pills. But what he really likes is the hum and thrum of people coming and going. Kids with coughs and concussions and cuts that need stitches. It's busy and vital and he likes the smell of the starchy sheets. Nurses come to take his blood pressure and his temperature. He feels safe.

Andrea looks up from her *Reader's Digest* and watches the boy on the gurney. His eyes have that slanted feral look of the bad boys she knew in high school. But not bully eyes. She knows bullies. This boy on the gurney does not look mean. Just lost. She is relieved when his dad shows up. But is it the dad? A coach? A social worker? She is curious. When the man leaves, Andrea pulls a chair up beside the kid's gurney and gets the whole story. His name is Cole, and he's a real storyteller.

Ryan died on Remembrance Day. It is coming up to Christmas now and Andrea is having a hard time getting her energy back. It is so dark and the days are so short that she has lost track of time. She has a campfire going in the back yard behind the shed. Down the ravine, she collects all manner of deadfall and birch bark and pine cones, then she feeds it to the fire. She is a fire-keeper and the fire keeps her alive. Ever watchful is the urn with Ryan's ashes. She drew owl eyes on it with a permanent marker and tucked it into the hollow of the oak tree.

The doorbell rings and Andrea traipses through the house to discover a boy on her doorstep. His face is shadowed by a baseball cap.

"Can I help you?"

"You don't remember me? From the hospital? I'm Cole." He lifts his arm, encased in a blue cast, to show that he can't shake hands.

Andrea remembers now. She met this kid in Emerg, one of the places she wandered to while Ryan slept. There she observed the steady stream of the sick and fearful. It was like a border crossing in the Middle East. The danger was that you could lose your passport and become an unwilling immigrant in a country of many hallways.

"You gave me your address. You said you had some clothes that might fit me."

Cole follows the woman. She is layered in sweaters and scarves and wears filthy fingerless gloves on her hands. They pass through rooms with dead leaves stirring in corners. He looks up to see if the roof is caved in or something, but it's not. At the end of a dim hallway she opens a door.

"Ryan's room. Help yourself," she says, handing him a gym bag to put stuff in.

He takes a Ti-Cat shirt and a hoodie and tries on a plaid jacket. It is a good fit. In the pocket his hand finds a stone, rough and cold. He pulls it out and examines it with interest.

"Trilobite," says Cole. "From before the dinosaurs. Did Ryan find it himself?"

Andrea opens the top desk drawer to reveal a box of fossils. Dozens.

Cole's face lights up. He runs his hands over the collection with undisguised admiration. "I guess he was smart, eh?"

"I guess. But he never did too good in school. He got bored easy."

Cole nods. He gets it.

"It's almost dark. Can I drive you someplace?"

Cole opens his mouth but says nothing. Andrea remembers his shaky voice that morning in Emerg, explaining about the pregnant roommate and the boyfriend. She realizes that he has no place to go.

"Oh, hell," Andrea says. "Stay overnight and we'll figure something out in the morning."

"But . . ."

"I insist."

"But I have a dog. She's tied up out front."

Andrea pulls aside the curtain and sees a sad-eyed mutt hunched against the fence. Ryan always wanted a dog. Begged for one. But those were the days when she used to vacuum and mop the floors. When she thought that cleanliness would protect them from decay.

"I've got a fire out back," she says. "We can cook her a hot dog."

The Happy Prince

The house tilts toward the gravel road, as lonely and spare as the woman who lives there. In the cab of his truck, Jamie is taking deep breaths, trying to decide how he can cut this visit short. He rolls the window down and listens. Silence. Not even crickets. Last week's hard frost took care of them for the season. It's as if the field of broken corn stalks is holding its breath. The only sign that he is still in the twenty-first century is a Canadian Tire catalogue in the ditch, offering a kick-start to Christmas decorating.

The lace curtain in the front window moves and Jamie pictures his grandmother watching him. She thinks he's an idiot. *Something wrong with that boy, Herb*, she is saying to her dead husband.

Jamie climbs the mossy steps to the back porch. The place is sinking into the earth like a decomposing pumpkin.

"Nana?" The old cat jumps down from the windowsill. "Nana?" Jamie flicks on the light switch and the florescent tubes cast a harsh glow over avocado countertops and harvest gold appliances. He leaves his boots on the mat and enters cautiously. In the front room, Nana is lying on the couch under a pile of shabby afghans.

She is dead. Looking. Dead-looking. Jamie dares to hope that this visit can be wrapped up quicker than he thought. Then her eyes open, and her mouth snaps shut.

"Water!"

In the kitchen, Jamie fills a cloudy glass with brown, foul smelling sludge. He checks the fridge. Nothing except a collection of aging condiments. He runs the water in the sink again until it is nearly clear.

"When's the last time you had your well checked?" Jamie asks as Nana drains the glass. He breathes through his mouth. The smell of urine is intense.

"Not sure," she says. "Can you do it?"

Jamie drives to town. He deposits two giant loads of sheets and towels at the Laundromat and goes shopping for essentials. The cashier at Foodland tells him in confidence that Depends are on for half price at Giant Tiger across the street.

It is midnight when Jamie slides between fresh sheets in his dad's boyhood bedroom. The faint trace of wood fire smoke drifts in through the ill-fitting window, making him nostalgic for slingshots and tree houses. Stuff he never had.

Nana looks better. Not health-wise. At ninety-two, there is no miracle recovery in the cards. But she is clean and she eats a bit of egg and toast. He is horrified to think that someone else may have found his grandmother, near death and neglected beyond human dignity. How long has she been like this? His mother visited in August and declared her mother-in-law to be fine. "Just stubborn. Age hasn't mellowed her any," she said.

"Can I drive you into town to visit your friends, Nana?"

"Call me Ruth, she says. When you say *Nana*, it makes you sound like you're five years old."

"So, Ruth, do you want me to call someone?"

"They're all dead," Ruth says. "Or they've lost it. Ann Wickham is in the lock-up wing at the lodge. The door is painted to look like a bookcase so nobody tries to escape. And Kate McLeod is at Sunrise Villa. Remember her? Maybe you could bring her out here on a day pass. She drinks rye and coke. Stop at the liquor store and pick some up. Pass me my purse."

For two weeks, Jamie does everything Ruth asks him to. He shocks the well, addresses the mouse issue, and puts a dehumidifier in the basement. The guys at the hardware store get to know him pretty well. On the second Sunday, he bundles Ruth up and takes her to church. They stay for coffee hour and Jamie enthusiastically accepts the offers, declined a hundred times before, of help. "Your grandmother is a firecracker," the minister tells him.

Church people start dropping in with muffins and banana bread. They put the kettle on and chat with Ruth. There is endless speculation about the new woman Reeve (not from here), complaints about the foreign doctor and dire weather predictions for the coming winter based on the observations of Harvey Ricker, the pig farmer. Pigs, apparently, are seldom wrong.

Jamie stays out of their way. He takes seven trips to the dump, levels the porch, and caulks around drafty windows and doors. After three weeks the locals are making fun of him because he keeps saying, "I'm on my way to California. Got a job waiting for me there. My friend has this company. Just going to clean out the shed and then I'll be heading out."

When he turns the calendar over to December, it alarms him a little bit. He's been here a month, and there are no offers to spell him off. His mother is in the middle of a creative period, just days away from finishing a series of paintings for a show at the Copper Fox Gallery. His dad is distracted, vaguely referring to some health concern that prevents him from travelling. His sister works full time and is raising two boys on her own. How fortunate that he is between commitments, they all say. How lucky for Nana.

On December 15th, Ruth looks out the window and sees the full moon. It snowed until about four o'clock, and the fields surrounding the farmhouse are as bright as day. "Let's have a bonfire," she says.

Grandpa's stash of split maple has been curing for five years. It burns clean and fragrant, sparks shooting upward in the windless night like sacrificed intentions bound for heaven. Jamie feeds kindling to the fire with a calm patience he hasn't known for a long time, and thinks about the wide plank pine floors under the linoleum in the kitchen. He could have them refinished in no time.

Mummified in her old snowmobile suit, Nana sinks into the camp chair. Jamie tucks a sleeping bag around her. They sit side-by-side watching the fire and observing the constellations. Ruth is sure that Cassiopeia can only be seen in the summer sky, and Jamie says, "No Nana it's the W, right there over the bush-line."

This is the best way to have a conversation, Jamie thinks. Without looking at each other. Like getting a lesson from your dad about condoms while driving in the car.

She tells him a few things about his grandfather that he didn't know. How he wanted to be an RCMP officer, but he was an inch too short to qualify. "Of course, nowadays they take anybody," she says. She tells him how Grandpa was careless with money. How he had an affair with their neighbor, back in the sixties. A hippie girl with dirty feet.

It gets late but she refuses to go inside.

"Freezing to death is supposed to be quite pleasant," she says. "Second in euphoria only to drowning. The Eskimos do it that way."

"Inuit, Nana."

"What?"

"Not Eskimos. Inuit."

"Oh for heaven's sakes. What's the difference? They put their old people on icebergs and shove them off. No muss, no fuss."

"I don't like the idea of explaining to the coroner that I left you outside all night."

"The coroner is Ian Smeltzer. He's an idiot. He just checks the *natural causes* box because it doesn't require any extra paperwork. Then he heads to the Queens Hotel."

"Well you're not dying tonight, Nana. Ruth."

"Don't tell me what to do," she says. "And pass that whiskey bottle over here."

"Whoa," Jamie says. "That's a big drink."

"Before I get too drunk, I want to thank you for coming here. I know you were on your way south. Every day you stayed on to do another job for me has been a blessing. I was a mess when you got here. You arrived like the swallow in *The Happy Prince*."

"Who's the happy prince?"

"You know. That story by Oscar Wilde? He was a homosexual like you."

Jamie grabs the bottle back and takes a hard swig. And then he takes another one. "You know I'm gay?"

"Of course. But who wants to talk about that? Sexuality is the least interesting thing about a person, don't you think? I'm sick of everybody making such a big deal about it. As if this generation just invented it."

"So, Oscar Wilde?" Jamie asks.

"I thought you were university educated! You must have read his novel, *The Picture of Dorian Gray*. Or heard of the play, *The Importance of Being Earnest*?"

"No."

"That's the problem with university education these days. It's no longer universal. Used to be you came away with knowledge in a variety of areas. Philosophy, sciences, languages."

Jamie supposes this to be true. His psychology degree is of limited scope, assessments of his learning based on multiple-choice quizzes. He is frequently embarrassed about his lack of knowledge on history and geography, and rarely ventures into conversations about politics.

"Oscar Wilde," Nana tells him, "went to jail for being morally corrupt. The most eloquent writer and conversationalist of his time, tossed in jail and left to languish. He died in his forties. Broke. He wrote the most poignant children's stories."

"*The Happy Prince?*"

"Yes, that was one of them. The prince wasn't so happy. He was a statue and he stood on his pedestal and saw all the poverty outside the castle walls. One day a swallow landed on his shoulder and this swallow was in a hurry to get to a warmer climate. Winter was coming and his friends were long gone. Sound familiar?"

"A little."

"But the prince asked him to stay and do some favours first. He was cemented in place, you see, and wasn't free to help those in need as he longed to do."

Nana pauses to clear her throat. Jamie leans over and wipes the drip from her nose.

"So the swallow took pieces of gold leaf covering the statue and delivered them to desperate widows and sick orphans and hungry artists. And then he plucked out the rubies and emeralds that decorated the prince's sword. Finally, he gave away the eyes. Blue sapphires."

"And then the swallow went south?"

"No. He'd waited too long. Besides, he couldn't bear to leave the prince helpless and blind."

"So, you think I'm the swallow? Well, thanks Ruth. But I'm not as altruistic as all that."

"Of course you're not. You're my grandson after all. Pass that whiskey."

Jamie wakes up on the couch with a dull headache. The house is cold. He gets up to pee and trips over a plate with a peanut butter sandwich on it. His heart sinks.

He pulls on his boots and heads outside. Beyond the last glowing embers, a shadowy lump reclines in a camp chair. Jamie starts rehearsing the story he will tell the coroner.

"Nana?"

Her eyes fly open and her mouth snaps shut.

"How long does it take to make a sandwich?"

The Chip Truck

Larry Logan is stretched out on a picnic table in Rotary Park gazing at the constellation Cassiopeia, the queen of the night sky. Her five bright stars form a W that stands for wisdom, or so Larry believes. He takes advice from Cassiopeia even though she was banished to the north sky as punishment for her vanity. Once she told him to go ahead and ask the new girl at the drive-thru for a date. That was a mistake. Maybe he misunderstood the message. It happens sometimes. Mostly she tells him to get out of this town and go someplace warm where people are nicer and all you need is a tee shirt and a pair of shorts. Larry has a fantasy of running into his dad on a beach in Florida. He took off years ago and left Larry with the mothball. That's what Larry calls his mother.

Now that spring is here, Larry can't sleep. He sleeps a lot in the winter, like a hibernating animal, but in the spring he is awake all night, with a buzzing in his chest that makes him restless. He has strategies to stop the buzzing, but he doesn't feel like using them tonight. Because an idea is starting to come to him as the stars fade into dawn. An idea that will set him free so he can pursue his destiny.

And then he sees it rising over the dollar store. Mars, red and fearless, is calling Larry to action. There's something out there, and he's waited long enough to go after it.

"So, I bought a chip truck today."

"What?"

"Larry's chip wagon across the road from the Legion. French fries. Onion rings. I own it now."

"No you do not."

"Yep, I do so."

"Bullshit, Harv."

"It's not bullshit. Larry got a call from Florida. His mother died. So Larry comes into the store with the keys to the truck and says, I'm leaving for Florida. Gonna live down there for a while."

"Larry gave you the chip truck?"

"Not exactly."

"What do you mean, *not exactly*," Edith says, reaching for the vodka she keeps in the freezer.

"Well he was all set to put a For Sale sign in the truck window with my phone number on it so I could deal with inquiries while he's away. And I says, how much are you asking for it? And he says, five grand."

"If you gave Larry Logan five grand for that greasy old fire-trap, I swear I will kill you right now," Edith says, grabbing a knife from the butcher block and pointing it at him.

"I offered him five hundred cash and he took it."

Edith uses the knife to stab at a bag of ice in the freezer and dumps a chunk into her drink.

"Are you insane?"

"I thought your brother could run it. Give him something to do."

"My brother can't even make his bed, let alone operate a deep fryer."

"You might be surprised what Jason can do if we get him out of your Mom's basement."

Harv owns the County Co-op store downtown. He sells seed and fertilizer and coveralls. It's Friday morning. He unlocks the door and takes a deep breath. The cedar floor has a patina of manure that the farmers have been bringing in on their boots for decades. Add the smell of leather and canvas, and you've got Harv's recipe for the best smell in the world. He flicks everything on. Lights, coffee and cash register in that order. By ten o'clock, a few farmers have wandered in to talk about blight and bad weather and the goddamned government.

At eleven, Larry Logan comes in, manic and shaky like he gets when he goes off his meds. He grabs a plastic For Sale sign off the rack by the front door and pulls a black magic marker out of his pocket.

"My business is for sale," he says. "The Chip Wagon is officially on the market. Spread the word." He explains how his mother has passed away in Florida, and now it's up to him to drive down there and get her stuff.

The farmers all mumble how they're sorry for his troubles, even though they know darn well that Larry never liked his mother much. Larry hands Harv a ring of keys with a wooden fish hanging off of it.

"So, Harv. Just in case I don't get back for a while, can I put your phone number on this sign as a contact? Technically it's a vehicle. Whoever buys it can tow it someplace or stay put. Five grand is what it's worth, but I'm open to offers. I'll call you from Panama City."

Larry scribbles Harv's phone number on the sign, even though Harv doesn't say anything to give him the idea that he is in agreement. "Appreciate it, Harv," Larry says, heading toward the door. His mother's old Crown Vic is idling in the parking lot.

"What'll you take for it?"

"You want it, Harv? Two thousand bucks."

"I got five hundred in the safe," Harv says. "Will you take five hundred for it?"

Larry owes Harv. Harv stuck by him when he got charged with animal cruelty back in the nineties. Larry never was too good at problem solving. He tied his neighbour's German Shepherd onto the back of his truck and took it for a drive down a gravel road after an altercation about stooping and scooping. Harv promised the judge that he'd keep an eye on him.

"Tell you what. You can have it for fifteen hundred. The taxes are all up to date and the freezer is full."

"Five hundred is what I got, Larry. Take it or leave it."

Larry pulls his cap off, a dirty old orange thing with a John Deere logo on it, and scratches the top of his head to help him think.

"You're killing me, Harv. But what the hell. You been a good friend."

"Is that high school kid still working for you on Saturdays? That Millie kid? The one that can run the place blind-folded?"

"Well, ya, she's still around. You might have to pay her some back wages. I was a bit short of cash last month and she quit on me. Kids got no patience these days. No loyalty."

One of the farmers rubs his hand hard over his mouth as if he is trying to force himself not to say something. Harv punches the combination on the little safe under the counter and pulls out an envelope.

"Is there some kind of ownership that you can give me? A license or something?"

"Taped to the wall behind the sink. And I'll sign a receipt right here, right now. We even got witnesses."

"I ain't watchin'," the tall farmer said.

"You want it or not?" Larry says, getting edgy.

"Sure. I can't even imagine what my life would be like without those onion rings."

"Deal, then. I'm glad to be shut of it." Larry stuffs the bills in his wallet and Harv walks him to the door and tells him to drive safe.

"Something don't add up there," one of the farmers says. "That lad's got himself in hot water is my guess."

Harv looks down at the fish dangling on the end of the key chain and notices two little x's where the eyes should be.

The group meets Thursday afternoons in the church basement. It's supposed to be a Bible study group, but mostly they just try to make sense of the younger generation. They all have grandchildren with learning problems and they all have adult children who can't seem to get their shit together. They call their group, "Anything Goes".

"I did not expect to have my forty-year-old son living in my basement. That is not how I pictured retirement," Martha says. She taught grade seven at the senior public school for thirty years and tuned up a lot of other people's kids. But not her own.

"I understand Jason suffers from depression," the minister says. She is new, a woman minister. You can't find men ministers these days. Maybe they have crawled into their mothers' basements.

"Well, yes he has depression. So did my father. He came home from work every day and lay down on the couch. I never saw him smile his whole life. But he *did* go to work. And he *did* pay his bills. You don't shirk your responsibilities because you have depression. It's the boys, it seems, can't rally from a patch of bad luck. My girls have all struggled one way or another and you don't see them giving up."

"Men," Betty Logan corrects her.

"What?"

"Men," Betty says. "You said boys. They're men. And yes, I agree. After he dropped out of that electrician's course, my Larry spent three years moping around looking like the town bum until I bought that chip truck. Bring in some dough or out you go, I told him."

The other women weigh in on their sons. They were not treated right in the education system. Ritalin was not a cure for ADHD. They got a bum deal when the plant closed down. They all would have fared better if they had been born forty years earlier when women didn't have more education than the men and wives were still supportive.

"I never thought I'd say this, but these boys might've turned out better if they'd had a war to fight," Martha says. "A year or two of being a soldier with bad food and bullets whizzing over their heads might have hip-checked their lofty expectations. I'm sick of all this entitlement garbage, like the taxpayers owe them a cheque every month just because they got the blues or some bad back."

Betty stands up and plugs the tea kettle in, and the minister, who was about to share some wisdom, decides to keep it to herself. She has met some of the sons. She has seen them around town, self-contained and suffering. The twenty-first century caught them off-guard. Now they are aging dreamers trapped between Main Street and the 4th Concession. But they don't come to church so she can't help them.

"They were such cute little guys once," Betty says as she puts the cups and saucers on a tray. "They all showed such promise, our sons." Betty feels her son's failure like a stomachache. When Larry was born, she was full of hope for him. But hope changes. She hoped he would be a doctor when he did so well in math and science in elementary school. Then, when he dropped out of high school, she hoped he might find a trade. When he was in his thirties, she hoped he might be able to keep a job for more than a week or two. She hoped he'd find a nice girl. She didn't even care anymore if the girl had been married before or had kids. Or if it wasn't a girl at all. Ruth Burnett's son was married to the church organist and those two men were the most successful real estate agents in Carluke County. Nowadays, she hoped Larry would have a shower and put on clean clothes without the humiliation of her having to nag him about it. Larry was a wound that just wouldn't heal. Even though she tried every kind of ointment you could imagine, Larry kept picking the scab off.

Harv drags Edith's brother, Jason, down to the chip truck on Sunday morning and they open the door to their new business. Edith was right. It is greasy.

"Don't light a match in here," Harv says. "You need a smoke? Smoke outside."

"AAAGH! Jesus! There's something alive in here."

"Coons maybe. Let me get the light."

"It's a dog," says Jason.

"Larry left his dog here? That's great. Isn't that just special?"

"I thought he wasn't never supposed to have any more animals."

"Larry's got a short memory."

"You'll have to drop this mutt over to the SPCA, dude. I'm allergic to dogs."

They prop open the windows and clean the whole place as well as two men who are not accustomed to cleaning can be expected to. They turn on the fryers and pull some bags out of the freezer. The whole place appears to be powered by a nest of extension cords that creep out the back window. Jason follows the wires past the porta potty and under the chain link fence until they disappear into a length of pipe that leads to a basement window of the United Church.

"Bugger's been stealing electricity from the church," Jason says.

"Well, we won't deal with that right now," says Harv.

"It's funny, eh? Larry was always griping about how much money his mother gives to the damn church, and here he is stealing it right back."

"That's your mom's church, too, you know, so don't be saying anything to her just yet."

"I don't never say nothing to her."

"Good. Keep it that way. Now let's get cooking. Put this on." Harv whips an apron at Jason. "When the oil starts bubbling, toss in the fries," he says, and then he goes out back to check on the dog. Some spaniel in him, it looks like. Must be half-starved. So Harv walks up the street to his store to get some kibble.

When he returns, there is a police cruiser in front of the chip wagon and Jason is leaning out the window shaking his head.

"He left town Friday morning," Jason tells them. When he sees Harv he tilts his head toward his brother-in-law and defers further questioning. "Here comes the new owner," he says.

"Betty's the owner," the officer says. "And she's missing."

"She's dead," Harv says. "Larry signed the chip truck over to me before he took off to Florida."

"Why'd he go to Florida?"

"Apparently Betty was holidaying down there. I don't know. All's he said was she was dead and he had to go down and tidy up her affairs or something."

The cops look at each other. "Betty's daughter claims she hasn't talked to her mother since Thursday around supper time. Says she was supposed to come over for dinner last night and didn't show up. Never said a word about Florida."

Harv pictures Betty, big bosomed and broad in the beam. She's one of those matronly do-gooders who fill Christmas baskets for the poor and volunteer at the local school, helping kids learn to read. She walks around town like her shit don't stink, complaining about the glue sniffers behind the arena and the graffiti on the old knitting factory. Poor Larry has always had a real project with her as a mother.

"Well, Larry's the one that lives with her, so I imagine he'd know best if she's alive or dead. The daughter lives over in Wainfleet, doesn't she? " Harv says.

"Jesus!" Jason says. "Smell that! Sorry to interrupt, but there is something seriously wrong with these fries."

Harv has smelled that odor before and he starts to get a bad feeling about his investment.

Sure enough, the ownership above the sink says that the business belongs to Elizabeth Logan. Or belonged to. By mid-afternoon there is crime tape all around the chip wagon and four police officers are loading the freezer onto the back of a pick up truck. Harv hears one of the local cops talking on the radio and wanders over to the cruiser.

"OPP picked him up at the Niagara Casino," he tells Harv. "He was living it up in a comped room. Appears he had a streak of luck with the money you gave him. And guess what? He was with a woman. Seems he found a girlfriend."

"The stars never did align for that lad."

"You are right about that. Probably half of the crimes committed in this county are by people who just have purely bad timing."

Harv looks over and sees Jason squatting in the parking lot like a refugee. He is smoking a Player's Light King Size with a trembling hand. Edith is pretty protective about her brother. She'll be mad. Time to go home.

"You okay?" Harv asks his brother-in-law.

"Yep. I feel bad about Mrs. Logan, though. And I want to get in the bath. I need to get this smell offa me."

"Didn't you notice they weren't fries?"

"I just thought they were, you know. Clumped together."

"I'm thinking it's time you move on, Jason. Go to the city and get a job. Even if you have to stay at the Y for a while, you don't want to end up like Larry. Living with your mother is no good."

"Ya. I've come to the same conclusion. What do you think I should do?"

"I don't know. Get a job. You're good at stuff."

"Ya? Like what? What do you think I'd be good at, Harv?"

"You could work with old people. There's an army of them marching toward the grave. They need somebody to feed 'em and play checkers with 'em and stuff."

"Ah, geez, Harv, no way. I can't deal with old people."

"Is that right?" Harv says. Jason hasn't noticed that his own hair is going grey. And he has a stoop to his shoulders that ages him. Sometimes, Edith says, people mistake him for her father.

"Well, there's a life out there with your name on it. What are you waiting for?"

Jason shrugs. He wakes up every morning, asking himself that exact question. *What am I waiting for?* He is waiting for the polar ice cap to melt. He is waiting for another meteor to hit, like the one that destroyed the dinosaurs. He is waiting for a disaster to release him from any potential responsibility. But the days disappear like the big bag of marbles that he got for his fifth birthday. They were perfect little galaxies trapped in glass with endless possibilities. One by one they rolled under the fridge. He got down flat on the floor with the wooden spoon and tried to retrieve them, but it was no use. The odd time, when he did reach one, he managed to knock it further away. Years later, when he was in high school, his mom bought a new fridge and when the guy from Sears pulled the old one away from the wall, there they were. All lined up between the baseboard and a curl in the linoleum, grimy and dull. Waiting for him.

My Life and Times

I suppose that in writing a record of one's life the chief difficulty must always be where to begin. To commence with the day of one's birth and carry on over the bridge of the years is not enough, for life's adventures really begin a generation or two before birth in the lives of those ancestors whose influences, like threads of many colours, weave in and out of the experiences and character of their descendants.

With that lofty introduction, my grandmother begins her memoir entitled "My Life and Times". The first entry is January 17th and the last is September 30th. It fills only the first twenty pages of the black leather-covered journal, leaving the great bulk of the lined pages blank. Either she did not have as much to say as she had anticipated, or the book was simply too big for the project.

That happens to me. My mind is exploding with a great idea. A novel, maybe. But when I empty my thoughts onto a page it is nothing. A few boring ramblings, unoriginal and poorly scripted. At least it gets the repetitive notions out of my head. Like deleting pop-ups on the computer screen, it works for a while.

Grandmother writes in spidery cursive in ink that goes from dark to light, dark to light. Dipping the fountain pen into a pot of ink must have been a very purposeful task. Her impatience shows in the number of blobs and scratches as she tried to load up the pen and then write until there was nothing except the very faintest trace of script. I imagine her, a big-bosomed imposing woman, sitting at the oak table that I inherited. Her family's story has been begging to be documented. Now, finally she has made the commitment. Bought the lined journal. Cracked the cover. She takes on this task with the same serious resolve she applies to everything, like changing the sheets on Mondays and canvassing for the March of Dimes. It has to be done, and it has to be done right.

"No nonsense," was Grandmother's favourite saying. "Now it's bath time . . . and no nonsense!" A visit to her house was not a holiday. It was more like a tune up. Posture, manners, grammar were all wanting in us, her children's children. No matter. If there was a problem, there was also a solution.

It seems more than a coincidence that I find Grandmother's memoir in this September of sadness as if she has returned to scold me. She represented that generation of formal ladies who wore hats and gloves and prepared Sunday dinners as if the Lord Himself was invited, using the good china and crystal and cloth napkins. The grandchildren sat around a card table dressed up with embroidered linen in the corner of the dining room, and were expected to behave. It is the ghost of this stern Presbyterian woman who rises up out of her memoir to grab me by the collar and give me a bit of a shake.

"You are not the first, nor the last to suffer, Laura," this ghost admonishes. "In fact, my dear, you come from a long line of sufferers who have born their crosses with dignity. This is my ancestral legacy to you. Listen well, Laura. Listen well."

January 17th, 1947   I can never, as long as I live, say enough in love and admiration for Mother. I loved Father. He had the gift of making his family feel secure and comfortable but, though he never was harsh with us, when he said step, we stepped. My mother had overcome the great disappointment of losing the family estate (called Manywells) due to Father's hot-headedness and his lawyer's mismanagement (or wickedness). She was forced to leave all her relatives and friends in England with five hundred dollars in pocket, five children to support and a husband who had no trade and had never in his life worked for anyone else. At eight years of age, I was the oldest child and the only one to recall vividly the miserable passage to Canada. My three sisters do not understand the demoralizing effect it had on Mother, as she always did her best to present a cheerful face despite the terror that must have been in her heart. She had a deep and abiding faith in the Fatherhood of God and I know that was what sustained her during those difficult years. I only once saw her give way to tears for she had always had firm control over her emotions. One day I arrived home from school a little early and found Mother with her head on her arms on the dining room table, crying. I was terrified ~ it seemed to me that the bottom had fallen out of my world and I slipped out quietly. I don't think she ever knew that I had seen her in her moment of despair. That was when we lived in the little cottage on Sheridan Street, our first home in Brantford, Ontario.

Grandmother would not approve of me, struggling daily to climb out of the deep well that is depression. She would never doubt that it is simply a matter of taking firm control over one's emotions. I can hear her voice repeating, "Never let them see you cry. Get firm control. That's the Gatecliff way."

I envy her abiding faith. Christianity could be a handy floating spar for a weak wretch like me. I picture my little ten-year-old self, sitting in the smooth pew of my childhood church, squirming uncomfortably as the minister lectures with stern assuredness. I count the rosettes above the vestry. I watch Mr. Adams in the pew in front of us clean out his ears. I cross my ankles in lady-like fashion and clasp my little gloved hands as I have been taught. I pray to Jesus to make the time pass quickly. I pray for a transistor radio so I can listen to the top forty hits on CHUM like my friend Wendy does. I am in love with Herman's Hermits and I repeat the words to "Mrs. Brown You've got a Lovely Daughter" until I hear the benediction. Then I wiggle in the pew to unstick my bare legs and get ready to leave.

When my daughters were born, I had them baptized and for years I attended the United Church that anchors the corner of Church and Main. It made me feel like a grownup, taking them in their little smocked dresses to sit on either side of me, the good mother. Then Reverend Black would summon the little children to come unto him, bribing them with a bird's egg or a stone or a leaf, something that demonstrated the wonder of God's world.

I sat alone then. Stuart worked Sundays. In those days he had two jobs. My track record of employment was starting to cause him some concern. The girls would file out of the sanctuary with the other little ones on their way to the church basement where they coloured pictures of Jesus healing the sick or getting his feet washed by Mary the prostitute. After the sermon, a nice quiet opportunity for me to be alone with my thoughts, the collection hymn would remind me to open my purse and place my envelope into the offertory plate. I was proud of the amount I managed to scrape together from my household allowance until a steward came to the house one evening and kindly informed me how much we really should have been giving according to our family income. Ten percent.

To add to my embarrassment, I couldn't make adequate contributions to potluck suppers. Apparently Rice Krispie squares, my specialty, don't qualify as appropriate desserts. When the girls started whining that they didn't want to go to Sunday school, that it was boring, I quit. For months, I expected someone to notice. To call and say, "Is something wrong, Laura? We've missed you."

No one called. No one really cared if I was there in the third pew from the back with my pathetic little offering. And so, after a year had passed I started researching different churches. Lately I have been sneaking into Roman Catholic masses and faking the sign of the cross. Also, Silver City has a New Age service on Sunday morning in the theatre. Comfortable seats. The pastor beams in his sermon from California and we watch him with 3D glasses. Very engaging.

I'm not totally incapable of taking control of my emotions. I've learned a trick. If I start the day with a shower, I will be able to function, to cope with the children, get them off to school, and perhaps even shop for groceries or throw in a load of laundry.

But if I run a bath upon rising, I know the day will be lost. It turns any momentum I may have gained overnight into self-doubt and free-floating anxiety. I forget things like dentist appointments and school concerts and feeding the pets. My working memory goes down the drain with the cold grey bath water. Surely Grandmother would sympathize, not with me, but with my long suffering husband who often comes home to find me sleeping, and the house a mess, and the children hungry for both food and attention.

January 20th *I must speak briefly of my antecedents as far as I know them. My father, Edward Pickels, born February 28, 1865, came of a long line of good yeoman stock. His father, Holmes Pickels, died at the age of 48 leaving my grandmother with a family of six to bring up alone, and all the large home farm of Manywells and several tenant farms to manage.*

I look up yeoman in the dictionary, and find it is a man holding and cultivating a small landed estate. A farmer, then, although I detect an element of snobbery in the term. A gentleman farmer, perhaps, whose employees do the manual labour. The tenants would provide an income, supposedly, while Great-Grandfather, smartly dressed with some accomplishment in literacy and numeracy, conducted the business end of the farm. Grandmother spends several pages painstakingly describing her childhood home, Manywells, in loving detail. The family's bankruptcy was her defining tragedy, though she was barely eight years old when they packed a few bags and left for Canada. You'd have thought she was the Queen of England by the way she went on about the squalor she had to put up with in Brantford.

January 23rd *My grandmother, whose name was Sarah Ann Baxendall was a tall, dignified woman who must have been beautiful in her youth. Although very slenderly built and with the most delicate features, she was strong and healthy and was said never to have suffered a day's illness in her life, save* *for the discomforts of childbirth and her last illness when she was seventy-two.*

This is the type of woman who Grandmother much admired and emulated during her lifetime. A stoic. Headaches, arthritis, these would not be considered worth mentioning. Even to the point of taking great pains to cover up any discomfort through strict discipline. Reading the diary, I am able to picture Great-Great-Grandmother Sarah drying roughened hands on a cotton apron as she surveys the farm from the veranda. She gazes at the vegetable garden and the orchard, then strains to recognize which of her six children are wading in the stream, and which are picking berries for the pie as they have been bidden. A white wash of sheets and towels and diapers obscures her view of the valley where the tenant farms nestle in relative poverty.

I see that she is just one woman, alone in the world. That she is just Sarah doing the best she can. Not because she wants to. No. She longs to travel to France. To read and paint and lie down in the afternoon under a soft quilt knowing that someone will waken her with coffee and beignets. She disguises her unhappiness and converts her anger into the fuel that propels her through one day and into the next. And silently, she curses Holmes who has gone and died and left her with all this to manage. Instead of pastoral beauty, she sees work. More work than she can cope with. Instead of household chores, which she can easily manage, she must now supervise the cultivating, the orchard work of trimming and harvesting fruit, and the stables. She has hired a fellow to oversee the tenant farms, but she is nervous about his reliability, even though the local parson recommended him.

February 2ⁿᵈ My father (Edward) was not overly strong as a small boy. He was subject to attacks of bronchitis, but grew sturdier with the years and I can rarely remember his being in any but the best health until the last two or three years of his life when he became the victim of pernicious anaemia. I have often heard what an accomplished horseman he was in his early days and that he learned to ride almost before he could walk. Upon the unfortunate advice of a friend, Sarah sent little Edward away to what she supposed to be a good boarding school. Evidently, the fees were high class but the school wasn't and apart from getting into plenty of mischief for which he was soundly whacked, he derived little good from his schooling. It is very much to his credit that he ended his stay there with as little harm as he did.

Sarah believes that she must send Edward, her firstborn son, away to school. He will learn to read and write and do mathematics and become a successful yeoman. But, like so many parents, she blames the school even though there is a good chance that her boy is not academically inclined.

Edward returned to Manywells and inherited the property when he came of age. But did he rescue his mother from her problems? No. Indeed he did not. He compounded them. For some unexplained reason, he gave the bulk of the property away to his younger brother, Herbert.

March 15ᵗʰ Herbert was a good-looking scapegrace sort of young man and I think rather difficult. He eventually sold the property, including the stone quarries, to Father's enemies, the Claytons, who built an imposing mansion with walled in gardens and imposing gates, known as the Manor House. Uncle Herbert was very foolish to let the quarries go as the Claytons made an extremely profitable business of them and there was no earthly reason why Uncle couldn't have done so. To add insult to injury, he married Clara, a pretty, irresponsible girl who made him a very poor wife. Clara was a poor homemaker, and refused to have children or be tied down at all and eventually became more and more involved with outside interests, the Suffragette movement, etc., and they were separated.

Ah! A heroine. I love Clara instantly and unconditionally. Great-Great-Aunt Clara the rebel. The rule-breaker. The Suffragette. And apparently she shunned housework, too. Grandmother cannot disguise her disdain for this woman who was the ruin of Uncle Herbert, even as she acknowledges that he was difficult and foolish. A proper wife, supposedly, would have known how to overcome these attributes.

March 27th *Uncle was one of the earliest motorcycle and motor-car enthusiasts and I can remember him taking part in a motorcycle race down Hemender hill and up the other side. In later life he worked for a motorcar firm as salesman. Unfortunately, after Clara left him, he tried to drown his disappointments and disillusionments in drink and for many years his family completely lost sight of him. What a wasted life and largely the fault of his wife. He died in very sad and impoverished circumstances five or six years ago.*

Tragic, I'm sure. Most likely, Herbert was a bum from the start. A charmer, mind you, but a bum all the same. And Clara was wise enough to cut her losses, no doubt, taking comfort in the strength of the women's movement. I envision her at a family gathering. She comes without a pie. It is Herbert's family, after all, and he certainly doesn't think of bringing a contribution for the picnic supper, but he would not be blamed for such an oversight. It is the wife's responsibility.

The real wives are in the kitchen, preparing the feast, minding babies, and taking turns at the window where they watch Clara, lovely in white linen. Hairstyle right up to date, she blushes and laughs as she plays at croquet with the young people. Surely Clara feels the poisonous glares, but she has built an armor of self-confidence that deflects the arrows so that they sting only the archers. Occasionally, when she catches a grim-faced matron watching her, she flashes a brilliant smile and waves carelessly. Intimately. As if she is so frivolous that she cannot discern the meaning of lips pulled tight and lowered eyebrows and arms crossed over ample bosoms.

Clara is not alone in matriarchal exclusion. Under the spreading oak tree, fanning herself with an exotic souvenir from her travels, is Jane, the ruination of dear Uncle Kingston.

April 3ʳᵈ *Uncle King entered the ministry and while in Ireland met and married a woman about 12 years older than himself and thereby signed the death warrant to his own life's happiness. We shall never know what fearful mental lapse caused Uncle King to do such a thing ~ her violent temper proved to be a terrible drawback to his ministry in Africa. He fought in the Boer War, during which time Jane returned to England. His house was burned down and he had some hair-raising adventures and some narrow escapes. Jane returned to him after the war, but her violent temper and suspicious nature became unbearable to our sensitive uncle and he left her and returned to England. He stayed with us at Manywells at that time, and we adored him,* *he was so gentle and lovable and had such a fund of amazing stories. But his brief respite from Jane didn't last. She found out where he was and insisted that he return to her. He gave up the ministry and went into business and for some years led a busy life of trade. Then he invented a soap for washing raw sheep's wool and it seemed likely that he would become a wealthy soap manufacturer. What happened, I do not know but it fell through and finally he returned to active ministry, though always held back by the burden of Jane's incurable temper and meddlesome ways. In the early part of 1901, we received word that Jane had died of pneumonia following a cold and that Uncle King planned to sell up immediately and spend his last years in peace in England. Our disappointment and grief were all the greater therefore when a letter from their landlady informed us that Uncle had caught cold and died of pneumonia less than a week after Jane's funeral. What a tragedy, just when peace and serenity were within his grasp. However, he is at peace anyway, where the wicked cease from troubling and the weary are at rest. It is a real delight to recall that long happy visit at Manywells, which Uncle always described as the happiest time of his manhood years.*

Oh boy. Here is the category I fall into, right Grandmother? Some women just do not know how to look after their men. Jane was shrill and demanding in her matrimonial unhappiness, trying to force it into functionality, whereas Clara became passive and aloof, seeking happiness elsewhere. Both were condemned for non-conformity and blamed for sending the uncles to early graves. They were poor wives.

I, too, make a poor wife, but I fear I am more like Jane, petulant and pathetic. A burden. Clara is the one I wish to emulate.

If only I could channel her confidence. If only I knew how to fill this aching empty place in my gut with her purposeful drive instead of vodka.

Years ago, when the children were babies, our washing machine broke down and I had to go to the Laundromat for a few weeks while we saved the money needed for repairs. I went in the evenings so Stuart could watch the kids. You would think that would have been a lonely time. The people drifting in and out, the tumbling towels, the futility of folding a load of clothes that will only get dirty again. But I loved those evenings. I read People magazines and met students who sat on the washing machines and drank beer. I helped an old widower who was confused and upset when his clothes didn't dry. When my washer got fixed, I was sad. Houses in the suburbs are lonely places.

Clara left. She looked around the lovely hills during that long ago family gathering at Manywells and thought, *I do not belong here. I will not be back.* Grandmother would surely be appalled at this alliance I have made with Clara. I am lost, but Clara calls out directions. Options. Possibilities. I hear her in the morning now when I wake up and she pushes me into the shower. "No," she admonishes when I look longingly at the tub, and she puts a picture there of a woman drowning. And the woman is me. I stand in the punishing pelting shower and I feel a little stronger than I did yesterday. It may be a mistake to pick up the memoir today, but I feel determined to complete it. Grandmother leaves off discussing her father's family and introduces me to her mother's side.

May 1st *(Grandmother Derry's Birthday) Of Grandmother Derry, whole chapters could probably be written but unfortunately those who knew her best have apparently left no written record. She was almost worshipped by her husband and children and she must have been a wonderful person because never once have I ever heard her criticized by anyone. She was small, slight, dainty, beautifully proportioned and with cameo clear features. Though Grandpa was stern, vain and forbidding and though she lived in an era when obedience to her spouse was a wife's main duty, Grandpa adored her. He called her his May flower and I rather think that he was ruled by her in her quiet gentle way more than he was remotely aware of. But though she often stood between the stern and arrogant father and his lively young ones, she was never able to prevail upon him to forgive the oldest boy, Frank, for his escapades and that was a sorrow she carried to her grave. Poor, darling little brave Grandmama with bobbing curls and beautiful care-lined face, how often must you have imposed your slight and fragile frame between your wrathful lord and his erring offspring, pleading their youth and high spirits as excuses for their misdoings. And how often your prayers and tears must have assailed the Throne of Grace on their behalf.*

Wow. Marriage was a struggle. Is a struggle. Then. Now. Grandmother devotes two pages to rationalize her grandfather's tyranny. He was handsome and something of a writer. He could even be humorous. The nasty side of his personality was expected behaviour in that era, I suppose. Men are kinder now. The expectation is that they will be kinder.

May 5th *Dear Papa in almost any family was tribal chief and oracle, and his authority not to be questioned. He died at the age of 74 after a stroke, or series of strokes, in 1895, the year of my birth. Grandmother died in 1897, of influenza during the epidemic that year.*

I close my eyes to think about this Victorian generation of stern husbands and obedient wives. I want to be called brave in my granddaughter's memoir. I vow to get brave. Today I will be brave. I will start with the kitchen.

But when I wake up, it is almost four o'clock and the girls are coming in the door from school and it is raining and their shoes are making a mucky mess in the front hall and the dog is barking and the backpacks are everywhere and everyone is so needy. They want me to listen, to solve something, sign something. Answer questions. What is for dinner? Where are my soccer shin pads? Can I have ten dollars for the book club?

When I start to cry, Annie hushes up. Katie keeps tugging at me, overly excited about an urgent matter, something about Open House and how many hot dogs should she order. Annie interrupts. "Wait for Daddy," she says, guiding her little sister upstairs.

I pour vodka into an orange Tupperware cup and take a gulp. Then I tuck it behind the pottery frog that holds the scouring pad, unused since Annie gave it to me last Mothers Day. Supper. Maybe if I was hungry, something would occur to me. But the thought of spaghetti makes me sick and the meat is all frozen hard. Soup? No. Eggs or pancakes or French toast? No. Stuart doesn't like breakfast at dinner. I take my copy of *Canadian Living* to the couch and hope that the Five Minute Dinners will inspire me.

But suddenly it is dark and Stuart walks in the door, calling out in concern. He turns on the lights, trapping me like a rabbit on the road. I go to bed and he makes some Kraft Dinner for the girls.

I wake up at 2 a.m. still clothed and lying on top of the covers. Stuart sleeps next to me, but he is under the comforter, snoring softly, turned toward the window. Slipping quietly to the bathroom, I drink some water and drop my clothes into the hamper. My housecoat hangs on the back of the door, inappropriately pink. I am not a pink person, but the robe is a gift from the girls and I wrap it about me thankful for it's heaviness. I tie it tight and turn out the light before I glide down the stairs to the kitchen.

The Tupperware cup is still hiding behind the frog and I add a little orange juice to it before joining Grandmother in her musings. On an impulse, I take the journal and turn on the porch light and go out into the balmy September night. Crickets cry as I read about the evil Claytons, those horrid people who bought the property from Uncle Herbert and proceeded to make great profits.

September 7th   *To return for a moment to the Claytons, who purchased that section of Manywells, the family estate, owing to Herbert's lapse of judgment. Prosperity did not bring happiness to that family. As the younger members of the family grew up they became wild and unmanageable, if indeed any attempt was made to manage them, as the parents were themselves heavy drinkers and of questionable morals. Fearful tales were told in the village of the wild orgies that took place in those lovely grounds. There was one child, born late into that ill-conditioned family, Mary, a red-haired, quiet, lady-like child and I seem to remember that out of that entire household of immorality and vice, young Mary* *grew to maturity, by some miracle, clean and decent like a lily in a muck heap.*

I think of my own Katie. Dark and elfin and full of the type of mischief that I seem to have no patience for. Once, as an infant she cried and cried and would not stop. All I wanted to do was sleep. I was exhausted. Annie was at school and I understood that the only way to achieve the peace that I needed was to hold a pillow over her head. I became very calm pressing the pillow. The pillowcase had little geese marching across it, faded because of the cheap detergent I used.

Quiet. It was so quiet, I could hear the refrigerator humming downstairs. I lifted the pillow, expecting . . . I suppose I expected to find her dead. But she was not dead. Katie looked at me with terrible knowledge in her eyes. A recognition that did not reveal panic or fear. She did not cry again that afternoon. Perhaps she hasn't cried since.

Sweet Katie is growing out of the muck heap that is myself. Childhood struggles are fertile ground for character, however. Fortunes can change dramatically in a generation. Katie might be the descendent that picks up the thread of Grandmother's tapestry, forging ahead through disappointments and loss and wading through muck heaps with all the self-righteous fortitude of the British Empire.

Grandmother was a loyal British subject in the days when seventy percent of the world map was coloured pink. Commonwealth countries. But the once-powerful empire has fallen on hard times and Grandmother's harsh voice, rather than criticizing me, has dissolved into a litany of whining regret. There is a lesson here, but no comfort.

A red maple leaf breaks from its branch and twirls grace-fully down to land on the last page of the leather-bound journal. Decomposing even at the height of its beauty, it curls closed as I watch, like Grandmother's arthritic hand grasping for me, desperately. I close the book and listen to the crunch with more than a little satisfaction.

Polio Camp

When the polio epidemic hit Carluke in the late summer of 1950, Mother was certain we would get it. She'd had a difficult childhood, lost a husband in the war, and when the black dogs of despair came scratching at the door, she'd lie down and let them consume her without a fight. She stayed with us, Betsy and Jimmy and me. But her commitment was casual, more like that of a cleaning lady who had been temporarily charged with our care. She had no relatives in this country, and she was suspicious of the motivations of others who may have extended some support, like church ladies or neighbours.

I did not worry that she would leave us alone, because even at twelve, I knew she did not have the energy to pack a bag. Looking back with a clearer understanding of our circumstances, I can see that motherhood was sheer drudgery for her. She was a romantic, I think, but lacking in creativity. Not up to the task of inventing parenting skills that might transcend poverty.

My mother's anticipation of disaster was usually rewarded. She would wring her hands and visualize something bad. Death, rent increases, blizzards. All of us growing out of our shoes in the same month. And so, when the school board declared that due to the high number of children falling victim to polio, schools would not open on the day after Labour Day as scheduled, Mother wept. She prepared herself for the burden of three cripples hobbling around the house with clacking braces on their legs.

We fully expected that she was right. We had come to understand that the pestilences were to be visited upon us whether we deserved them or not. Constructed after the First World War for returning soldiers, our house was part of a dilapidated assemblage of dwellings only slightly more comfortable than the trenches. Perhaps the government of the time assumed the poor buggers were too damaged to notice the inferior quality of the gesture. Besides, they needed all the money they could get for the dead. Cenotaphs were costly.

Reduced to sipping whiskey out of a brown paper bag on his front steps and pissing into the forsythia bushes at the back of the property, our neighbor, John McKay was off limits for us. Not unkindly, Mother told us to leave him alone with his troubles. Until that September, when we were forced to suffer through the heat wave, we'd never had a conversation with him. But waiting for polio to strike us down made for a long day. Television would not arrive in our living room for ten years. The pools and beaches were closed. Even the library was locked up.

I felt responsible, being the oldest, for keeping us all busy. We played school, ran races, burned up an anthill with a magnifying glass. We invented a game of treasure hunting and we drew maps, with X marking the spot. We buried small items for the others to dig up. A spoon, a tin can, a toy soldier.

By noon on the third day we were tired and cranky and hot. The weather was relentless. As long as the heat continued, polio would stalk us. Then, out of pure frustration, I invented Polio Camp. I made Jimmy and Betsy lie in the iron lung, a thistle bush that they had to creep into and out of with extreme caution. I supervised their therapy, forcing them to walk from the front gate to the road without bending their knees. I predicted their shortened life span and said a prayer for their immortal souls, sprinkling grass over them as they were laid to rest in their graves. Tragic. John McKay was watching.

"Hey. C'mere," he said, summoning us over to his front step. He cleared his throat and hawked a great gob of spit over his left shoulder. We sidled up to him, ready to run if need be.

"You ever been to the woods?"

"No." I spoke for the three of us.

"Never?"

"Nope," Jimmy said. "Never."

"Would you like to go?"

We looked at each other. Of course. Of course we would like to go to the woods. We nodded.

"Ask your mother."

We ran in the house. Mother was standing in front of the sink, running cold water over her wrists. She didn't mind cold water in this heat.

"No," she said. "What are you thinking?"

"It will be cooler there," Jimmy said.

"You can come too," Betsy said.

Mother got that far away look in her eyes that made us believe she was consulting a long dead relative. "Okay," she said.

We couldn't believe our luck. The woods were not far, but they were forbidden to children. We didn't question the restriction.

We had read Hansel and Gretel. We knew the stories of wolves and other predators. We knew that a child could lose his way and end up in quicksand.

John McKay, it turned out, was not always drunk. He looked drunk. But he was quite sober as he guided us down into the valley, pointing out the names of plants and trees. He led us to a stream, cool and clear, and told us we must take our shoes off and enjoy the feeling of clay between our toes. My mother did not protest. She seemed relieved that someone would tell us what to do. Take an interest. John McKay had played here as a boy and he remembered the secret places that he and his chums had discovered. There was a beech tree and a maple tree that had grown together with their limbs entwined like lovers. His initials were carved on the beech.

"Here," he said. "J. M. and E. L. My girlfriend. Elizabeth. She swore she'd wait for me when I went off to war, and she did, too. Wrote me letters. Sent me dry socks that she'd knit herself. But she took sick. Imagine that kind of shitty luck. She died of the flu in 1919."

We followed a deer trail back into a copse where there was a little waterfall and we sat on the limestone ridge at the top and let the water redirect itself around us. "You can't do this in April," he said. "We'll come back in the spring and you'll see. It will be rushing over like Niagara Falls."

We stayed in that sanctuary until a barred owl hoot, hoot hooted and John McKay led us back up the trail and across Mrs. Mishook's orchard and onto our dusty street. With the moon rising, our little kitchen window with the lace curtains looked almost welcoming.

John McKay promised to take us back the next day.

"We'll go every day," he said, "until school opens again. When the teacher asks what you did these long dreadful days, you will tell her you were at Polio Camp." He smiled. He had been watching us play. He had been paying attention.

The days were quietly delightful. We learned about the great struggle, as John McKay called the First World War. He had been propelled by an exploding shell into a cement wall. The blast cracked his skull and left him deaf in one ear. It ripped his friend's right arm into shreds and the field doctor had to saw it off above the elbow. *Sawbones.* That's what they called the doctors back then. No disinfectant. He got the gangrene. And he died.

My mother had rolled her stockings down to her ankles and tucked her skirt up under her knees. She listened and did not object to these stories that were, of course, too lurid for children. These were days of reprieve for Mother, from the sole responsibility that burdened her. Having a man, a grandfatherly man, call us by name and compliment us on our behaviour, well, it helped her see the good in us, I think. It helped her see the possibility that we would grow up one day and be able to care for ourselves. He started to call her Lydia and gave her some ideas on how she might improve her lot in life. There were nursing schools and teacher training academies.

"You'd make a lovely teacher," he told her. "If I was a student, I'd be happy to sit in my desk and look upon your sweet face." She blushed and we saw that, yes, our sad mother was transformed in the mottled sunlight that fell through the green canopy.

"Daddy died, too," Betsy told John McKay. "His grave is in France. We can't visit it. It's too far away."

"I know, my love," John McKay said. "And I am beyond sorry for your loss."

We were all quiet then. No one had ever expressed sorrow to us. We felt the reverence of it. The sheer comfort when someone acknowledges your pain.

John McKay had been a scholar with a Doctorate in Philosophy, he told us, and he missed his opportunity to be a professor. He didn't have the energy, after the war, and after Elizabeth died. But he told us about the great philosophers and quoted the Greeks.

"Hope is a waking dream, Aristotle said. Now, what do you think that means?" John McKay would not let us shy away from voicing our opinion. "It takes practice to say what you think," he said. "We are all afraid of ridicule."

He coaxed us and encouraged us and even Mother was made to tell her ideas. John McKay found strength in our arguments. He would nod and pause and digest our words as if we were gathered in the agora, pondering the complexities of the universe.

"Give yourself some think time," he advised. "Don't talk for the sake of talking. Mull it over. I'll come back to you."

When we were reluctant to answer a question for fear of being incorrect, John McKay taught us that you could never be wrong if you prefaced your ideas with *in my opinion* . . . "Your opinion is yours," he said. "Yours alone. And you can take that to the bank."

After that, Mother called him Professor and he didn't tell her not to. He brought a book with him one day, a book about war, and started reading it aloud. *The Red Badge of Courage.*

It was about a boy who went willingly to war and then found he couldn't get out.

"War is a waste," he told us. "All that sorrow from my war, and no one learned any lesson at all. The young men could hardly wait to head off to Europe again in 1940. Nothing that I, or any of the other old soldiers said, could make them believe that they would be nothing more than ammunition for powerful ambitions."

Mother had an opinion. We were surprised and interested in how articulate she sounded. John McKay had opened up a little hole in the dyke and all the frustrations and discouragement that had been debilitating her came flooding out.

"Aristotle is wrong," she declared boldly. "Hope is not a waking dream, but a waking nightmare. My waking hours are filled with frustration and envy. I watch all the veterans in this town, friends of my husband who at one time had lesser prospects than he did, and I see them in well paying jobs or attending university paid for by the government, and their wives and children are living in brand new homes. The whole country is buoyed by the optimism of victory and the assurance that their efforts have been successful. Parades. Celebrations. Hitler is dead. Japan is burnt to a crisp. Everything is going to be all right. My husband made the ultimate sacrifice and all the Department of Veteran's Affairs can tell me is go home to England. You should be with your people. What people? They were bombed out in the blitz. They all died."

Of course, we knew they didn't all die. Her Great-Aunt Molly offered for us to come and look after her. But we also knew that our mother would rather live in squalor in Carluke than crawl home to the dementia-rattled bitch who had punished her with a switch when she was a girl.

So, Mother continued in a voice choked by emotion. "Instead of getting a brand new bungalow on Cross Street or Park Street or Fairview Street, instead of living near the new school and Lion's Park with playground equipment and a pool, instead of having neighbours who are doctors and teachers and chartered accountants, we are relegated to a row house on Water Street with the likes of you, John McKay, and the other poor old buggers who put up with drafty windows and leaky roofs. And they expect me to be grateful! Oh, for the wall-to-wall carpeting in the new homes. What wouldn't I give for the convenience of a washer and dryer and a hot water heater. And an indoor toilet."

John McKay nodded. He rubbed his hand across his whiskery mouth. He did not jump to reply, but waited until his words were thoughtful and wise.

"You have stated your case, Lydia. There is much injustice in the world, but no one is going to come around and seek you out and ask if you are satisfied with your life. You are perfectly capable of changing it. Look at your neighbor, Mrs. Gaspari next door, for instance."

Mother never spoke to Maria Gaspari. She considered herself to be of a better class than the Italians next door.

"Mrs. Gaspari," John McKay said, "keeps a big enamel pot of hot water on the stove for washing up. She never complains about the lack of a hot water heater. She accepts what she has. Mr. Gaspari's uniform is always clean and pressed when he leaves each morning for his caretaker job at the hospital. They are saving for a home on Park Street. They will be moving within the year."

My mother was flustered. She looked at us and saw what others saw, three dirty kids with dirty clothes. Perhaps if we had an enamel pot of hot water at the ready on the stove, we could scrub our faces before school in the morning. Mrs. Kettle, the grade two teacher, had humiliated all three of us by keeping records of dirty fingernails and grubby ground-in neck grime and greasy hair. She had failed us all in personal hygiene. Mother had just shrugged and said, "What does she expect? We live in a coldwater flat."

The next day, Mother didn't join us in the woods for Polio Camp, and John McKay didn't either. "You are all trained as campers now," he said. "You must go and blaze your own trails." We were happy to do it. We headed down into the cool valley and waded in the clay bottom stream and polio did not find us there. When school opened on September 30th, we were healthier than we ever had been. And cleaner.

That fall, our mother was like a campfire with accelerant thrown on it, full of blazing anger and purpose. She marched into Veteran's Affairs and demanded all the benefits that would have been our due if our father had survived. She got everything she asked for. By Christmas, we were living on Forest Street. We had a driveway too and when Mother finished her nurses training (paid for by the government) and started working at the hospital, she bought a used Mercury Meteor to park in it.

On the first Christmas Eve in our new home, our new doorbell rang. Betsy and Jimmy and I all ran to answer it. It was John McKay, with a stack of presents looking like a ragged Santa Claus.

Mother came out of her kitchen wiping her hands on a little red apron with candy canes stitched onto it. "Come in, Professor," she said. "Merry Christmas." We sat around the yellow laminate kitchen table and opened the gifts. *Jane Eyre* for me. *Of Mice and Men* for Jimmy. *Anne of Green Gables* for Betsy. *To Kill a Mockingbird* for Mother.

We thanked him as kindly as we could manage, with only the faintest traces of disappointment in our voices. They were used books, well worn and smelling of our old house. But he had thoughtfully inscribed every one of them with words of encouragement.

I read my book. I read Jimmy's. I read all four and re-read them. Sometimes when I want comfort, I pick one up and open it and take a great whiff of the yellowed pages. Wherever I move, they move with me. How strangely pleasant stories of hardship can be. The language of loss is a dark cloak that never fails to warm me.

I don't know if Mother ever properly thanked John McKay for the kick in the ass he gave her at Polio Camp, but I am sure he got some satisfaction out of seeing our pictures in the local paper when we graduated from high school, honour students all. While an epidemic crippled and killed thousands of North American children, we received our vaccinations in a green valley where the maple and the beech embrace and keep each other from falling to the forest floor.

Wind Chimes

After a long winter and a late spring, Leah's window is open to the lovely smell of dirt and worms and reawakening grass. She looks at the lighted dial on her bedside Big Ben clock. Three-thirty. Damned if she will shut her window just because someone has hung discordant wind chimes to torture the neighbours. They are drilling into her brain like a spike of black cancer.

That idiot Wayne, next door, was raking his yard yesterday and she noticed he set out his hideous frog family lawn ornaments. The wind chimes, no doubt, belong to him.

Leah gets out of bed with an angry spurt of energy that temporarily blinds her. She stabs flabby arms into the sleeves of her housecoat and steps into matching pink mules.

The wind chimes are coming down. The wind chimes are about to meet a terrible end. Leah feels like a gunslinger in an old western as she descends the narrow staircase and opens her back door. She takes a few tentative steps out into the night, crossing her arms over her bosom and craning her neck. Listening. Listening. *Where are they?* The wind chimes taunt her like the students in her short-lived teaching career.

Leah was not successful in stopping the undignified behaviour of thirty-five grade seven students. They refused to listen as she presented her carefully planned lessons on Canadian history. They chatted and rolled their eyes as she recited events that led up to the Rebellion of 1837. "This is on the test!" she screamed at them.

At Christmas, the principal suggested she would be happier in some other profession, and indeed, the controlled environment amid the stacks of the university library were more suited to her disposition. *Delicate*, her father had called her.

"You're my little hothouse flower, Leah," he'd tell her. And it was true. She needed to follow a routine. She couldn't tolerate harsh foods. No onion or garlic or hot peppers for her! She listened only to the soft strains of classical music, cringing whenever she entered a shopping mall where they were likely to blast popular tunes at unassuming customers.

The wind stirred the dark cedars that separated Leah's yard from Wayne's. Her slippers sank into the mud as she sneaked through the hedge.

"Hello Leah," Wayne said.

Leah jumped. Wayne Henderson might have been a vampire for the scare he gave her. He was sitting on the wooden bench on his back patio, wearing a sloppy sweat suit and smoking a cigarette.

"Those infernal wind chimes are not mine, I assure you. In fact I thought they were yours. I've already checked your backyard and the Arnold's and the Kovacevic's."

Wayne had lived in this house for forty years, arriving with his young bride, Sylvia, in 1965. Sylvia left him to live in some artist's colony on Vancouver Island after their daughter grew up. Leah hadn't spoken to Wayne in ten years. Not since he cut down the oak tree that was on the dividing line between their properties without asking her permission. Her father, God rest his soul, had planted that oak tree.

"Oh, well then. I need to track them down," Leah stuttered. "I intend to lay charges. Is there not some bylaw?"

Wayne swallowed a great gulp of scotch from a silver flask and stood up. "I'll accompany you, Leah."

"There's no need," she said, turning away from him.

"I insist," he said. He flicked the brown filter, still glowing, into the freshly turned earth of his garden and followed her through the back gate to the laneway. They walked in silence toward the lake. Toward the cacophony. The moon was waxing just past halfway, bright enough to cast sinister shadows.

"The moon was a ghostly galleon, tossed upon cloudy seas . . ." Wayne quoted aloud.

". . . and the Highwayman came riding, riding, riding . . ." Leah replied, in spite of herself. High school memory work. She took a sideways glance at Wayne. "How old are you, Wayne?"

"I was born in 1939," he said. "August seventeenth."

"Oh. I thought I was older than you. We're the same age. Actually, you're several weeks older. I was born in September."

This is the longest speech Wayne has ever heard his neighbour give, aside from the maniacal rant she delivered after that oak tree incident. It cost him five hundred bucks to hire a surveyor to prove to her that her crotchety old dad had planted that oak tree on the wrong side of the property line.

The lane curved and dipped down a sandy embankment to the beach road. Cottages lined both sides. The waves of Lake Huron crashed rhythmically on the shore. Still, they did not drown out the sound of the wind chimes. Wayne paused long enough to take another swig of scotch and observe his quirky neighbour marching on ahead. A square little body in a pink housecoat with grey hair caught in a long braid halfway down her back. She turns, suddenly, and he is surprised to see the flush of her cheeks, the bright excitement of adventure in her eyes. Leah waits for him to catch up and then leans in toward Wayne's shoulder.

"We're very close now," she says.

Wayne nods. He wonders where you can buy the sort of wind chimes that make such a racket as to rouse old people from their beds. He is frankly amazed that there are not hundreds of outraged villagers closing in with torches and sharpened pikes.

The laneway delivers them to Point Clark, where the lighthouse flashes its warning and the wind whips Leah's housecoat so high she is reminded that she has no underwear on. In the adjoining park, a tent has been erected. A big tent with flapping flags like a circus. It looks like a living thing, breathing in and out.

"Must have been a wedding," Wayne says.

"Of course," Leah says. "I read about it in the paper. The Johnson girl married a boy from Owen Sound. A dentist, I think."

Wind chimes hang at the entrance.

"Those aren't wind chimes," Wayne says. "They're pipes. Goddamned hurricane pipes."

Inside, centre pieces of spring flowers and wine bottles anchor white linen to a dozen round tables. Bus trays full of dishes and cutlery are stacked on the head table.

"I feel like we've come upon the ghostly ruins of a failed civilization," Leah says, grabbing a half-full bottle of red wine.

Wayne sits down in a linen-covered chair and crosses his legs. He lights a cigarette with a tiny plastic lighter that looks like a toy.

"I was married in the month of June," he says. "We were married in Sylvia's mother's garden. There was no tent, though. I don't know what we would have done if it had rained. Sylvia locked herself in the bathroom the first night of our honeymoon and cried herself sick."

It has been years since Leah has had an intimate conversation with a man. His remembered anguish is somehow attractive. She wonders what it was about Wayne that repelled her so. This man who spent thirty years in the profession that she had failed at.

"I'm sorry about the oak tree, Wayne. I get a lot more light in my front window since its gone." It is the only thing she can think to offer him.

Wayne takes a deep drag on his cigarette and wonders about this reclusive spinster librarian who peeks out between her lace curtains, furtive. Suspicious. The neighbours blame her eccentricity on her miserable old father. The Professor, people on the street called him. Not because he was a professor. He was a manager at the Royal Bank, but because he was a nasty old know-it-all who claimed that his ancestors were United Empire Loyalists. He must have written a thousand letters to the editor over the years, whenever Canada made a move away from the monarchy. When the Canadian flag replaced the Union Jack and when "O Canada" was sung at a town event instead of "God Save the Queen" the local paper published his diatribes.

"I should have warned you I was about to cut the tree down, Leah. It's just that, well, I avoid conflict. That's one reason Sylvia left me. I guess. Neither one of us could bear an argument so we just simmered and stewed until we were too mad to fix it."

"Whatever became of her?"

"She's an artist. Caroline tells me she makes cement sculptures of people with huge hands and feet."

"Caroline. Your daughter. What is she up to?" Leah has found a box of clean stemware and is pouring red wine, marveling at how wonderful it looks in the goblet, like a cup of blood in some medieval legend. She swirls it and brings it to her lips.

"Caroline lives in Calgary. She has two boys. Hockey players."

"Well," Leah says. "I would've liked to have had a family."

Wayne squirms in his chair. He is uncomfortable with such talk. "Well, anyway, you did right by your father. You took care of him. You were a good daughter, Leah."

"I was a fool. I should have left when Mother did."

"Your mother left?" Wayne assumed the mother had died before he moved in next door. He had always pictured a woman beaten down by the old tyrant. A woman who welcomed the respite of her grave.

"Yes. When I went to Teacher's College, she packed her bags and moved to Toronto. Worked at Simpsons down on Queen Street. The toy department of all places. She went to the theatre and the art galleries and had a gay old time."

"Why did you stay?"

"I don't know. I was angry, I guess. Angry at the wrong person. I sided with my father, you see, who railed against my mother for abdicating her duties. I rushed in to take her place. To placate him. I did everything. Laundry, grocery shopping, cooking, cleaning."

Wayne watches as Leah finishes her wine and refills the glass. She empties it willfully, like medicine. He wonders if he will have to carry her home, or maybe go get the car. Suddenly she jumps from her chair, lifts the wind chimes off the hook and dumps them unceremoniously in a Styrofoam cooler.

"He started to call me *Mother*. I wasn't even thirty yet, and he was calling me *Mother*. I was still hoping . . . I mean, I know everyone at the library assumed I was destined to be an old maid. I turned down invitations to go to the pub after work. I had to go home and get Father's dinner on the table. He'd get agitated, you know, if he didn't eat at six o'clock sharp, and then I'd pay for it. He had a temper."

Leah shakes her head. Then she strikes off, out of the tent, down past the lighthouse and clambers over the rocky ledge to the lake. It is all Wayne can do to keep up with her. He thinks she means to drown herself. By the time he reaches the shore, Leah has pulled her housecoat off and yanked her nightgown over her head, flinging the garments wide as she wades into the cold waves.

Wayne gathers her clothing and stands helplessly watching. This is more drama than he is accustomed to. His heart is pounding in crazy half-beats. He is torn between waiting for Leah to come out and running to call 911. This is why people carry cell phones everywhere, he realizes. But then, seeing the strong arms arcing in a brilliant backstroke, he sits on a rock and decides to wait it out. He tips the last of the scotch into his mouth and remembers skinny-dipping with Sylvia, diving off dark piers in leaps of blind faith that he could not manage now. He is too fearful. His brittle bones are awaiting any excuse to snap. Still, he has to admit he is tempted. Instead he scoops a handful of cold, pebbly sand and lets it sift through his fingers.

Leah emerges from the surf like a goddess, enchanted and powerful. Wayne hasn't seen a nude woman since Sylvia left and he is taken aback by her lack of self-consciousness. The wine, he thinks. She lets him help her into her housecoat, threadbare and smelling of mothballs. He feels as casual as a gentleman helping a lady into her coat after dinner at the club. The nightgown he rolls into a ball and tucks under his arm. They walk home in silence, not close together, but no so far apart that their arms can avoid a bit of gentle jostling as they step over the uneven bits of the path. Leah's hair drip, drip, drips behind them like a trail of temporary madness.

Wayne escorts Leah right to her door.

"I'm not at all tired," she says as Wayne turns to walk down the steps. He hesitates, wondering if this is an invitation, and if it is, how can he respond in a way that won't hurt her feelings? He longs for the parameters of their former relationship. He wants the crabby old Leah back.

"I should have brought along another bottle of wine," she says. "How much would a bottle of wine like that cost, Wayne?"

"Less than ten bucks," he says, smiling. It had been an inexpensive wine from Niagara Falls. "But, I think come morning, you won't be in a big hurry to drink wine for a while. Take two aspirins and swallow as much water as you can before you go back to bed. Oh. Your nightgown." He tosses it to her, afraid to take a step in her direction. Afraid to encourage her.

"He got confused. He believed I really was Mother," Leah says. "He started to bother me at night and I had to barricade myself inside my bedroom. It was terrible. Most times I was able to evade his advances but once I had to punch him. I gave him a black eye."

Wayne is at a loss as to what he should say. How can he respond to this disclosure? "I'm sorry, Leah. I'm so sorry for your troubles," he says.

"I almost killed him one time. He was feeble and bedridden and I was feeding him some Cream of Wheat. And the old bugger reached over and ran his hand up under my skirt and dammit! I smashed that bowl over his head. He went limp. I left the room and didn't go back in until morning and, well, I was disappointed to find him still breathing. Tough old bird. Tough old dog."

Wayne nods. "Yes. He was a tough old son of a gun." Then he turns and walks home.

Leah takes Wayne's advice immediately, but she is not tired. She gets a towel from the linen closet, unbraids her hair and gives it a good hard rub. Hanging the towel up, she hears a thump at the front door.

The morning paper. She retrieves it and notices the eastern sky brightening where the oak tree used to be.

Rural Route

Grace Shaver

It's hard to know what kind of a person can be successful in a small town. By high school, you can start to guess at who might go on to enjoy a decent life, and who might end up a total failure. Then, there are the ones who leave looking for money or fame or anonymity. Lots come back, disappointed in city life.

If you are going to stay, you better come to terms with the fact that no one is ever going to let you forget about the time you peed your pants in grade two. Or the humiliation you endured at the Christmas Dance. You better just wear that cloak of shame and understand that everyone else has one, too. If you are too sensitive, or if you try to switch your cloak for one that you like better, you might as well go to the city where nobody gives a shit.

A small town has a long memory. Not that it can't be forgiving. It doesn't expect you to be perfect. Not anywhere near. I remember laughing with some friends about Peepers, the old guy who sat on the steps of the post office all day sipping at something in a paper bag. By late afternoon, he'd have a stain down the front of his pants. My dad set me straight.

"Grace," he said. "That man was brilliant, once. Before he went off to war, he was a math teacher. But when he came back, he wasn't right in the head. Not his fault. He's a drunk. But he's our drunk."

After that I started to notice the way people treated Peepers and it was a good way to figure out who had integrity and who did not. I watched the pharmacist cross the street go and sit with him one day, and share a sandwich. And shake his head in agreement with something that Peepers was saying, like maybe about the weather, or some memory about how the town was in years gone by. Kindness gets noticed, same as meanness does.

I had my own troubles as a young girl. Got married too young and lost a baby in a fire and ended up looking after my mother who had some mental issues. But looking back, there was always somebody in this town that cared enough to give me a hand up when I needed it. Grant McCarthy at the school board got me my job at the elementary school as the secretary twenty years ago and I never forgot that trust he had in me to take on so much responsibility.

A school is a good place to read the future of a community. There are fewer kids here now than ever before. We've got three empty classrooms this year. A hundred years ago when the river was the main thoroughfare for moving goods up to the city, this town was booming. A family could still make a good living at farming, and there were plenty of jobs at the cannery. It was seasonal work, but if you were a fast packer you could make enough in a few months so it was worthwhile, and then of course collect pogey in the winter.

Folks who had got along well enough on the assembly line found they had no skills for other jobs when the cannery closed. Crystal was part of that leftover generation of families immobilized by a changing culture of work. But Crystal had some gumption. I tried to help her a bit. I saw she had at least a ghost of a chance.

Crystal McIntosh

The smell of manure enters the classroom so suddenly, so stealthily, that all twenty-three grade six students are gagging at the same time. They glare accusingly at Ken vanOsch, whose father owns the pig farm half a kilometer down the Indian Line. Ken does not acknowledge the odour or the stares except for the smallest hint of red around his shirt collar, a collar that is starched and buttoned up to the top, even in the muggy heat of early June, giving him an old fashioned look. A ghost of a pioneer boy, out of tune with his peers. He sits tall in his seat and follows Mrs. Ricker's geography lesson with a frown of concentration.

In row six, two seats behind Ken, Crystal McIntosh sweats. The tall windows drown her in harsh sunlight, just as they tortured her all winter with icy drafts that kept her silently shivering. Before electricity, the windows were meant to let in enough light for the children to read and write, but no school architect ever sat in row six, trapped in a desk that was bolted to the floor, through frost and dampness and heat. A poor design.

Crystal, as a name, is poorly designed for a girl with greasy blond hair, pulled back in a rat's nest of a ponytail. The backs of her hands and her elbows and knees have the kind of ground in dirt that takes years to accumulate. When the lice check mothers find about ten thousand nits in Crystal's hair, they are disgusted. Mrs. Wendall, who volunteers for nit-picking and hot dog days, claims she has never seen so many on one head.

Sitting on a bench in front of the office, six cootie-heads wait for their parents to be called. Mrs. Shaver, the secretary hates lice check day. She hates to break the bad news to parents. Your child has head lice. Your day is now ruined. You will have to cancel all plans and go to the pharmacy and buy the expensive shampoo that will kill the lice. But that is only Step One. Then you will have to pick out the nits, those tiny eggs that stick to strands of hair like Crazy Glue, one at a time. There are thousands of them and if you overlook even one little white egg, it will hatch and start the process over again. So be vigilant.

By noon, five of the children have been picked up. Mothers have gathered up babies and left laundry undone. Fathers have excused themselves from work, mumbling about illness. One grandmother gave up her euchre game at the church when the parents could not be located and reluctantly accepted responsibility.

Shame, shame, double shame. Their faces all wear the mask of humiliation as they enter the school. Mrs. Shaver knows them all. She has lived in this town all her life and she is careful to treat them with respect. She gives them a paper from County Health that tells them what to do. Shampoo, vacuum the rugs and the upholstery, pick out the nits, change the sheets, throw out the stuffed animals. Wait three days. Shampoo, pick out the nits, vacuum, change the sheets, and on and on until you are dreaming about lice. Until you are checking your family's heads like orangutans at the zoo.

"Dippity-doo," she whispers as they go out the door. "I used Dippity-doo when my grand-daughter got the head lice last year. After you shampoo and comb out the nits, just slather on the Dippity-doo and leave it there for a few days. If you missed any nits, they can't go anywhere when they hatch. They get stuck in the goo and die." The people are grateful for this advice. They are grateful to hear that Mrs. Shaver has had head lice in her family. A good Baptist and a member of the hospital board.

Crystal sits alone. Her scalp is itchy. The back of her neck is itchy. She stares at the dirt under her fingernails and wishes she were dead. When Mrs. Shaver calls Crystal's house she gets a message that says the phone is not in service at this time. Doris, Crystal's mother, has neglected to pay the phone bill. She is a woman who has not coped well after her husband lit out. Mrs. Shaver takes a deep breath and pulls her lunch out from under her desk. She opens the Tupperware container with carrot sticks and another that has dip and she munches away while she watches Crystal through the little glass window that makes the office look like a take-out restaurant. Crystal feels Mrs. Shaver watching her. She lifts her eyes reluctantly and tries to meet the secretary's eyes with as much dignity as she can muster, which is not very much.

Grace Shaver opens her little office window.

"Have you got any lunch, hon?"

Crystal shakes her head, no. She usually makes herself a jam sandwich, but it is near the end of the month and there is no grocery money left. Bread is all gone.

Mrs. Shaver opens her sandwich Tupperware. Honey ham on whole wheat.

"You like ham?"

"Yes, ma'am," Crystal says.

"Here you go," Mrs. Shaver says, holding out a triangle and smiling. Crystal does not move.

"Come and get it, hon. I'm not scared of lice."

Crystal rises with the posture of an omega wolf. If she had a tail, Mrs. Shaver thinks, she would have it tucked between her legs. She takes the sandwich and says thank you without making eye contact.

Mrs. Shaver wonders what to do about this problem. The principal is at a meeting down at the board office and she doesn't want Crystal sitting in the front hall for the rest of the afternoon. After a few more bites of carrot, she buzzes the grade eight teacher and asks for a student volunteer to answer the phone for an hour. She grabs her purse.

"Come with me, hon," she says. "We'll go get some shampoo. Have you fixed up in no time."

After luxuriating in a hot bath and using the bug killer shampoo, Crystal finds herself seated on a stool in Mrs. Shaver's backyard, watching bits of her blond hair fly away on the breeze.

"Always pick nits outside," Mrs. Shaver says. "It is easier to see nits in the direct sunlight, and besides, the nits will fly off and hatch in a field somewhere, not inside the house." Crystal looks into the middle distance and watches a ginger cat lick himself in the shade of the forsythia bushes.

"That cat is twenty years old. A hundred and forty in cat years. Imagine a person living to be that old?" Mrs. Shaver says as she drags the fine-tooth comb through the short hair at the back of Crystal's neck. "This is where the lice like to lay their eggs. I know it hurts, hon. Scream if you want to."

But Crystal does not scream. She is thankful that someone is touching her. That she is not as repulsive as she feels. Lilacs are bursting with a fragrance that Crystal, even into her old age, will associate with kindness. At one o'clock Mrs. Shaver calls the school and tells Emily, the grade eight student, that she won't be back until the next day.

"Do you mind getting your books and working at my desk for the afternoon? Oh, thanks, Em. You're a good girl. I owe you one."

Crystal pictures Emily Anderson sitting at Mrs. Shaver's desk. She is not one of the popular grade eight girls who go to the city to buy their clothes. The ones who lean against the bicycle racks and laugh in a shrill way with their heads together, making you wonder if they are laughing at you because you are skinny or fat or a have a birthmark. Things you can't help. Emily is a reading buddy and a kindergarten helper and a crossing guard and she once helped Crystal find her winter boots that someone had buried at the bottom of the lost and found box.

"I bet Emily will be a teacher one day," Mrs. Shaver says. "She is such a responsible girl. There are not many grade eight girls I would let into my office, I tell you."

Crystal hopes that she will be the office helper when she gets to grade eight. She sits statue-like as Mrs. Shaver thins out her hair and takes a few inches off the bottom.

"I wouldn't be surprised to see your hair in a lot of bird nests this year, Crystal. For every bad thing that happens, a good thing is bound to happen, too. Those birds are getting some fine material for their nests, you see? They're pleased as punch you had to have a bit of a trim."

Crystal is wearing one of Mr. Shaver's tee shirts that covers her knees, like a dress. Mrs. Shaver puts Crystal's clothes in the washer with Javex.

"That's what you must do with your sheets and pillow case tonight, dear. Wash them in hot water with a cup of bleach. Then vacuum your whole house."

Crystal nods her head in understanding, but something in her quiet acquiescence gives Mrs. Shaver pause.

"We don't want to go through this again, do we, hon?" So Crystal gets the Dippity-Do treatment, which is slathered through her hair like pink Vaseline and then, topped off with a bandana.

"Keep it on for three days." Mrs. Shaver says.

That night, Crystal takes and burns her pillow and the dingy flannel bedspread that has been passing for sheets. She watches the campfire, imagining the lice curling up and dying. She flips her mattress over and sprays it with the heavy-duty bug killer from the shed and that night, she sleeps out in the back seat of the 1966 Impala, baby blue, that is up on blocks in the garage. Her head itches unbearably. She would love to take off the bandana and sink her fingers into the Dippity-do, and scratch her scalp until it bleeds. But she does what Mrs. Shaver tells her.

Crystal gets her clothes from a musty room in the basement of the United Church, castoffs from rummage sales. The first Thursday of each month, the room is open from four until six for those in need to come and help themselves. It is guarded by two church ladies who whisper disturbing bits of news to each other about sick people and funerals. But, for all that, they are a good-natured pair. The tall one is called Gladys. She has a high-pitched voice and calls Crystal *dear*. The other lady, Marlene, is shorter and rounder and she calls Crystal by name.

"Here comes our best customer," Gladys says as Crystal walks in. Practiced in the kind of casual conversation that Crystal admires but has never mastered, the church ladies ignore her, mercifully, as she roots amid the wool and denim and damaged polyester. She avoids items with food stains down the front, but other than that, she has learned not to be too picky. Underwear and socks are bonuses.

The church ladies have started to set these personal items aside in Crystal's size. Sometimes they suggest she take a sweater for her mother, or a sweat suit for her brother, Roy. Today she shyly inquires after bed linen and is rewarded with flowered sheets, a soft pink blanket and a pillow.

"They look like they've never been used, Crystal," Marlene tells her with excitement. "Maybe someone bought them for their guest room and never had any company."

When Crystal gets home, she sorts out her wardrobe. Dirty clothes from last month's scavenging go in the garbage. They don't own a washing machine. Not one that works. There's an old rusted-out machine on the porch, but it never was hooked up as long as Crystal can remember. Her father used to drive Doris to the Laundromat in town once a week. Her mother didn't drive. She lost her license before Crystal was born.

Crystal peels some potatoes and puts them on the stove. She likes how potatoes fill her up. While she waits for them to cook, she climbs up to the loft. The loft is her room, away from her brother Roy who wanders in the night, looking to snuggle up to something warm. Which has gotten to be a problem since he's nineteen, now. A man. With hairy legs and hair on his inflamed face and a need to rub his crotch up and down on whatever's handy, like furniture, or a tree stump, or a little sister. Crystal woke up one night last summer with his heavy bulk weighing her mattress down. She jumped out of that bed like it was afire, and never went back. She pulled her mattress up into the loft along with a few necessities, and then she invented a way to pull up the ladder into the loft with her. Not that Roy could likely manoeuver himself up the ladder anyway, but Crystal knew she wouldn't sleep until she could be sure.

She doesn't blame Roy. Hell, he still pees himself like a little two-year-old. It seems to Crystal that Roy has gone downhill since he graduated from high school. The Life Skills program gave him someplace to go every day. There is an adult program that he qualifies for, but Doris told them no, Roy wasn't going to go and make birdhouses with a bunch of retards. Crystal thinks anything would be better than sitting around all day in this dump but she knows better than to disagree with Doris. Since Doris took to her bed a few months ago, Roy hasn't even had a shower or clean clothes.

"Make sure Roy's got something to eat," Doris pleads in a defeated, whiny voice that makes Crystal feel like slapping her across the face. "And don't let the town take him away."

As if the town would want him, Crystal thinks, but doesn't dare say it aloud. Dealing with her mother is like walking on eggshells. All spring, Crystal has been in charge of the cheque. She is careful to pay the rent first. Then she goes straight to Foodland to pay off the tab. Mr. Andrews, the owner, is happy that Crystal has taken over managing the money, and he tells her so.

"Your credit is good, here, Crystal," he says. She likes praise, and feels duty-bound to deserve it. She feels proud going around the store with her grocery cart and filling it with bread and potatoes and pasta and cheese and apples and peanut butter and milk, carefully avoiding chips and pop, anything that would get the town gossiping about how that welfare family, the McIntoshes, blow their money on junk food and liquor and cigarettes.

She refuses to buy her mother cigarettes, but while Crystal was at school one day, Doris got sneaky and had them delivered by the drug store. Crystal was furious to learn, back in April, that she owed Smith's Pharmacy forty dollars and change for cigarettes. She cleared that up right quick with the pharmacist. No more deliveries to the McIntosh house on the Inman Road. Crystal would pick up any supplies that were needed. And cigarettes would not be among them. The pharmacist briefly considered calling Children's Aid, noting on the computer that Crystal was only eleven, but decided it was more trouble than it was worth.

Crystal leaves Roy's food on the table, where he will find it when he is hungry, like a dog. He comes and goes from the house, favouring an old fallen down garage out back, but does not leave the property. When he wandered off one time to the farm next door, Mr. vanOsch pointed his shotgun at him and then, turning it upward, fired off a few shots, giving Roy such a scare as to teach him a lesson. The vanOsches have a pond and they are scared Roy might drown in it.

Crystal likes the vanOsches, and they like her. Ken, the oldest boy out of four brothers, is in her class and they sometimes team up for projects, wordlessly gravitating toward each other when Mrs. Ricker says, "Find a partner." He is serious and respectful of others, even when it is not reciprocated. His manners are impeccable. Mrs. vanOsch occasionally sends Ken over with a casserole with some kind of pork in it, since they own a pig farm.

Crystal thanks Ken and sometimes he sticks around for a game of Scrabble. Ken has a plodding way of doing things that Crystal finds reliable. He has what her teacher, Mrs. Ricker, calls *high moral fiber*. If you cut him in half, you would see that he is high in fiber. Like bran flakes or whole wheat bread. Ken is a boy that will be a good farmer. A good community man. A good church-going man. His family attends the Dutch Reformed

Church on the Seventh Concession and they go five or six times a week. He will be a good husband, perhaps a little too strict with his wife and kids like Mr. vanOsch tends to be, but that is considered responsible behaviour over at the Dutch Reformed Church. Ken will be good all his life. Never great. Even Crystal senses he is not smart enough to become great. But he will always be good. He will not leave his family for a far away job. He will not marry a girl who likes to drink and smoke and flirt with car salesmen. His choices will always have the measured thoughtfulness that he gives to his Scrabble tiles.

Crystal leaves her mother's dinner beside Doris's bed. Sometimes the food gets eaten, and sometimes it just goes to waste, shrinking and darkening and hardening until it often becomes impossible for Crystal to wash up the dish without soaking it overnight. Orange cigarette filters pile up in an aluminum pot that Doris slides under her bed, hidden from Crystal's criticism. She has stretched her precious carton out to last six weeks, but she is on her last pack.

Crystal takes her own dinner up to the loft and does her homework as good as she can manage. Good enough so Mrs. Ricker can see she's tried. Crystal knows the "good enough" rule. She knows what she can do and what she cannot do. She does not waste time feeling sorry, like her mother. Doris has given up, it seems. Lying in a bedroom that has a funky smell of unwashed hair and dirty sheets and stale cigarette smoke. Crystal doesn't know who to blame. Her father for leaving them, or her mother for driving him away. Crystal remembers her dad as a quiet man with shoulders stooped from hard work. He would sit at the dinner table and chew in silence as her mother complained about having no money. About how she should have married Eddie, the captain of the football team that she dated in high school, who's in real estate now and making a ton of money.

"I could be living in that nice new survey over by the hospital," she'd say. "Instead of in this shack."

Crystal was surprised how hard her mother took it when her dad left. Doris didn't seem to like him much anyway. Spoke mean to him all the time. But she was in the habit of blaming him for her disappointments and when he wasn't around there was no one to blame but herself and Doris wasn't willing to do that. She didn't have the capacity to grit her teeth and get a job.

Crystal means to get a job as soon as she is old enough to work part time after school. Not babysitting, either. Or farm work. Real work. With a real paycheque. She will apply at the drug store and at the grocery store. She will apply at the pizza place and the hospital cafeteria. Maybe she will work two jobs, or three. She will put her money in the bank until she has enough to rent an apartment in town that has hot running water and a bathtub like Mrs. Shaver's. She will clean it with Comet and hang fluffy yellow towels on the towel racks.

"Crystal," people will say, "your floors are clean enough to eat off of."

At the June head check, Crystal sits nervously under the nit picking sticks of Mrs. Wendall who sounds almost disappointed when she says, "Clean. Next."

Mrs. Shaver waves Crystal into her office and slips a butter-scotch candy wrapped in gold foil into her hand. "Good girl," she says and Crystal gets a hard lump in her throat so that she can't reply, only unwrap the candy and suck it thankfully as she walks back to class.

On the last day of school before the summer holidays, Crystal walks home with her report card. She is proud to be passing into grade seven. She stays back to sign up to be a lunchroom monitor for the primary students in the fall. A position of responsibility. On her way home, the siren goes off. The number of siren blasts lets the volunteer fire fighters know where the fire is. Two blasts is the north end, three blasts is the east end. And so on. But the siren stops at one blast. That is a drowning. Mostly, the drownings are at the dam where fishermen sometimes lose their footing on the slippery algae-covered bottom. She thinks maybe it is Roy, drowned in the vanOsch's pond and she hopes that it is. Then she is disgusted with herself and prays to god that Roy is all right.

The house is different. As soon as Crystal climbs the crumbling porch steps she knows.

Doris is gone. Her black leather purse is gone. Her good shoes, the green suede ones she bought for Aunt Becky's wedding five years back when Crystal was a flower girl, gone.

The cheque.

My god. Crystal realizes it is the twenty-fifth of the month and the mailbox flag is down. She runs out to the road and pulls open the battered silver door. It has been crooked since a wild bunch of high school kids bashed it in with a baseball bat last summer. Empty.

The mailbox is empty and the cheque is gone. Gone. Crystal grieves for that cheque. The cheque is hers. Her responsibility. Her power.

Roy. Crystal remembers the siren and runs to the back of the house to look for Roy. She hopes that she will not see him. She hopes he is drowned in the pond. She imagines the status that she would achieve in town as the unfortunate sibling of a drowned boy.

And where is Doris? Maybe, informed of the death of her son, she was roused out of her stupor. Maybe she is identifying the body. Maybe the cheque is still in her purse and Crystal can get it back. All these thoughts fly through Crystal's mind as she looks in the empty garage and runs around back of the old barn. Her heart is beating in anticipation of change. Then she sees him. Roy is crouched over the body of a long-dead cat, flat and dry as cardboard. It has been there for weeks.

"Suppertime?" Roy says in a slurred dialect that only Crystal understands.

"No, Roy," Crystal says. "Don't touch that thing, Roy. Dirty."

As she turns to walk back to the house, Crystal dares to hope that it was her mother that drowned. She would be an orphan. Maybe Mrs. Shaver would adopt her. But Crystal knows in her heart that her mother does not have the moral fiber it takes to throw herself over the bridge. More likely Doris finally got up enough of a craving for cigarettes and vodka to get her out of bed. She has probably planned this for a while, waiting patiently for the twenty-fifth of the month. Crystal smacks her forehead, angry with herself for not anticipating this crisis. She pictures Doris marching off down the road in a short skirt and the green high heals, sticking her thumb out. Smiling.

Crystal props up her report card on the sugar bowl and puts her head down on the sticky oilcloth that covers the kitchen table. When she finally opens her eyes, the sun is slanting through the kitchen window, harsh and hot. Roy is sitting beside her, rubbing her back with a hand that is surprisingly gentle.

Doris McIntosh

Doris squints into the June sunshine wishing she still had that pair of Ray Ban sunglasses that she stole from the Rexall Drug Store in Wasaga Beach summer before last. The old five finger discount. Doris was an expert, rarely got caught. And when she did, she just flashed her violet eyes and the manager would let her off with a warning. What happened to those glasses? Maybe Al took them with him when he lit out for the far north, promising to send a paycheque. Promising to call every Sunday. *Asshole.*

As she reaches up to shield her eyes, she is alarmed to see how white her arm is. How thin. Hearing a car approaching from behind, she whirls around and sticks her thumb out. One woman, all alone in that big old van and she can't be bothered to give a neighbor a ride into town. *Stuck up bitch.* That wouldn't have happened ten years ago. Town was friendlier back then. Now if it had been a man, Doris is sure he would have stopped. Doris never did get along with other women.

Doris swaggers along the gravel road in her high heels. She is starting to get a blister. In her own mind, Doris looks pretty good. She would be surprised if she knew that Anne Jenkins who drove past her in the van had taken in the teased up hair and the black leather halter top and wondered what a heroin addicted cross-dresser was doing in Tory Hill.

Doris takes a sniff at her armpits, wishing that she had thought to wash. She tells herself to pick up some deodorant after she cashes the cheque. Deodorant and some hand cream or body lotion. Her skin is dry and scaly. And bandages for her heels, which are now a sticky mess, blood seeping into the dark green suede attracting a very persistent horse fly.

Mascara. Doris is also low on mascara. But more important is a carton of Player's Light and a twenty-sixer of Smirnoff. Then she will enjoy herself for a change. Nobody has any idea what she has had to put up with. When Al left she went through a bad spell. She lost the will to live, so to speak. Nothing seemed to be worth the bother of getting out of bed. So she decided to do what her mother did, turn her face to the wall and pass away quietly in the night.

Doris has more respect for her mother now that she realizes that dying isn't an easy thing to do. You can feel like dying. Wish death upon yourself. But the actual dying part is tricky. Maybe her mother had been sick all those years after all. Her papa had let on that her mother was faking it just to get out of doing her share of the work.

"Oh she's sick all right," he'd say. "She's got the L-A-Z-Y- disease. Woman never lifted a finger in all our married life. Never cleaned a toilet. Never cooked a decent meal. Never kept up with the laundry. She may be the first woman to die of pure laziness."

Home was a trailer that her papa had bought off a guy in Peterborough who got it from a circus fellow that went bust. A bunch of animals took sick and the strong man killed a guy at a bar in Bancroft. Doris loved her papa, even though he was unreliable as a parent. An Irishman who could spin a good yarn, he sometimes told a story so often that he was more disappointed than anyone else to find that it was not true.

"Fuck off!" Doris yells at the horsefly that is tormenting her tortured heels.

"That any way to talk to an old friend?" A white pick up truck pulls alongside Doris, and as the dust settles, she recognizes the leering grin of Billy Watson who got her pregnant in grade ten and then denied up and down that he was Roy's father.

"Coulda been anybody, darlin'," he told her. "I got friends on the football team can testify you been a busy little girl." Which was unfair, as she was a cheerleader and cheerleaders were supposed to date football players. But the night they lost the playoff game to Coboconk High, Doris passed out in the back of Jamie Simpson's Volkswagen van. She woke up bruised and battered and definitely deflowered. But not pregnant. It was Billy that was Roy's father, all right, but Doris didn't know there was a way to prove it. Instead, her survival skills kicked in and she managed to hook up with Al Hill, an older guy, who tended bar at the Vic. With her breasts all swelled up from being pregnant, it didn't take a whole helluva lot of convincing to get Al to propose. The joke was on her, though, in the long run. *Asshole.*

"Get lost, Asshole," Doris says, opening the truck door and hopping up onto the sticky seat.

"Still a real lady, I see," Billy says. "I was just on my way down to Pinky's to quench my thirst. Join me for a cold one?"

"If you'll wait five minutes while I run into the bank," she says.

"Why sure, darlin'. You know I'll wait as long as it takes."

Roy McIntosh

Roy watches Crystal as she opens a can of Alpha-Getti. She pours the red slop into the small pot and puts it on the stove. Crystal is his sister, but she takes care of him, and he can tell when she is upset about something. She is not saying it, but Roy knows it is true. Crystal goes quiet when she is mad. Not like Mom. When Mom gets mad, you better run for it! Doris has swatted

Roy more times than he can count. Sometimes it is for spilling his milk or peeing his pants, but mostly it is for ruining her life.

"I wished you woulda never been born," she yells.

What Roy does not know, was too young to remember, is that Doris shook the shit out of him when he was seven months old. She was the first one to admit she had no patience with a crying baby, least of all after she'd had a few drinks. That kid picked the wrong time to start howling and Doris let him have it. He jerked around and his eyes rolled back in his head, but it wasn't anything to worry about. He had pulled out of it two or three times before. Besides, there wasn't any help to be had with Al out of town on a job and the phone company cutting off her service again. So she just put him back in his crib and passed out.

Roy was dead in the morning. Or so Doris thought. While she was making up a story for the cops about how he must've fell out of his crib during the night, she heard a noise. A weird sort of cry like an animal would make. Doris picked Roy up at arm's length and took off his reeking diaper. She tried not to look at his face as she washed him up and zipped him into a terrycloth sleeper. Then she put him back in his crib and went next door to get help.

Except that, on her way to the vanOsch's house, Eddie Myers drove by on his way to school. All of Doris's friends were still in school.

"What are you up to?" he asked.

"Just going next door to borrow a cup of sugar is all," Doris said.

"How about we have a little visit first? Get caught up?" Eddie said.

If it had been anyone else except Eddie, Doris told herself later, she would have said no. But she had her eye on Eddie ever since Orientation Week in grade nine when he grabbed her ass while she was getting a book off the top shelf of her locker. Eddie with the soft brown cow eyes and the messy hair that made him look like he just rolled out of bed. Before she knew what was happening, Eddie was driving past the high school and they were on the lake road.

"Don't you have classes to go to?" Doris asked.

"I can go to class anytime, darlin'. Today I feel like spending time with you."

Eddie parked down by Grass Lake. He took her hand and walked her down to an old dock. They sat and dangled their bare feet in the water and watched for snapping turtles until the liquor store opened. Then Eddie bought a bottle of rye and a few cans of coke and they drank all afternoon in the backseat of his father's Cadillac.

Back in the dim shadows of his bedroom, Roy spent the day going in and out of consciousness.

Eddie dropped Doris off at three o'clock. He had to go to football practice.

"When will I see you again?" Doris asked as Eddie pulled up to her mailbox.

"I'll call you," Eddie said, barely slowing down.

"My phone's out of service," she said. But Eddie had already leaned over and closed the passenger side door and peeled off like the devil was chasing after him. *Likely worried that Al might find out*, Doris thought. She went straight to the couch to lie down. She had a wicked headache. Rye did not really agree with her, she'd have to tell Eddie that next time.

It was midnight when Doris woke up, thirsty. She stood at the sink and drank three glasses of water and then caught sight of her own reflection in the kitchen window. It hit her then. The thing she had forgotten to do. She went and lifted little Roy out of his crib. He was limp and heavy on her shoulder. She went next door, waking the vanOsches who called an ambulance.

Roy survived, saving Doris from a manslaughter charge. Survived that and went on to nearly getting killed a second time when Doris threw him in the car two years later to make a late night run to get cigarettes. The cops said she was going well over one-twenty when she caught the soft shoulder just this side of Town Line and over-corrected. Flipped the vehicle twice before it landed in the ditch, ramming the cement culvert so hard that Roy was thrown halfway up the Richardson's front lawn. Drunk driving. Driving under the influence. Lost her license.

"Should lose her parenting license, too," one of the nurses at the County Hospital said as she bundled up little Roy, preparing to send him home after two weeks in intensive care.

It nearly broke Al's heart losing the Impala. And, if Roy had been his kid, he likely would have watched out for him more than he did. Maybe he'd have tried to find a job closer to home. He made a poor choice getting taken in by Doris and her lies. But then, he had been less than honest with Doris, omitting to tell her that he couldn't have any kids of his own. Shooting blanks, as they say. He got sterilized by the red measles when he was a teenager. So when Doris got pregnant with Crystal, he just smiled and acted pleased and stopped feeling guilty for having a girlfriend up in Fort McMurray.

Garbage Day

Edna leans over the sink and clears away her angel collection. She grunts as she opens her kitchen window. It is April, bleak and damp, but mild enough to let in some fresh air. The grackles are making a racket in the cedars and her neighbour, Marie, is taking the garbage out. Edna pulls the dishtowel off her shoulder.

"Did George die?" she asks.

Ralph looks up from the Letters to the Editor. Pastor Travis has written a convincing argument for the corporal punishment of young children.

"George who?"

"Next door George."

"George died?"

"I don't know. That's what I'm asking you."

"I don't know. The ambulance was there, when? Thursday night?"

"Marie's cleaning out the garage. Come here and look. She's dragging all George's flea market crap out to the curb. Here she comes with another load. There goes that wine rack he got at Larry's yard sale last month. It's a really nice wine rack."

"I know what you're thinking," Ralph says.

"Don't flatter yourself," Edna says as she squirts Sunlight dish soap into the soup pot.

Ralph glares at the back of Edna's grey head. "We have a wine rack already and we never use it. It's covered with dust in the basement. We don't even drink wine for Christ's sake. One thing we don't need is another wine rack." He shakes his head, wondering how he ever married a woman who loves knick-knacks so much. He cannot stand clutter himself. He cannot stand Edna's clutter.

"Still. It's a nice one. I might go over there and have a look at what she's throwing away. All the stuff George has been carting home since he retired, it's all going out in the garbage. Do you think he died?"

"If he died, I didn't hear about it."

"Call your sister. She knows everything that goes on over at the hospital. Ask her."

"You call her if you want to know. I don't really care, one way or the other."

"You never liked George, did you?"

"I liked him fine, but I'm not sorry he's dead."

"I don't know if he's dead or not."

"Well, if he's not dead yet, he will be when he sees that his wife threw out all his stuff. He was going to open up a little second-hand store or something."

"Maybe I will give your sister a call."

Ralph folds the paper and tries to find where he left off with Pastor Travis. He likes what the Pastor has to say about strapping. He got the strap himself as a boy, and he believes the world might be a better place if kids got the odd pounding. The slugs, kids used to call it. The principal called your name over the PA system and you went down and cooled your heels in the chair outside his office, getting more nervous the longer he kept you waiting. Some of the older boys called it the heater. And it sure as hell did heat up your hand. But it never killed anybody. And nobody wanted it a second time, although there were kids who got it again and again.

Edna scours the soup pot with an SOS pad, watching out the window the entire time.

"If he's dead," Ralph tells her, "he hasn't made the obits yet."

"Here's a car pulling up. A little grey car. Who drives a grey Saturn? Oh, look, Ralph, it's the daughter. What's her name? You know. The one that used to be a lesbian but she's not anymore. Jennifer or Jessica. Something like that. A "J" name. It must be serious if she's come all the way from out west."

Edna hangs her apron on the hook by the side door and grabs her green cardigan. She buttons it up and steps into her Crocs. "Back in a minute," she says.

"Don't be bringing any garbage back with you," Ralph says.

"So, is he dead?"

"No. He just had a stroke. Can't say but four words. *Did the Leafs win?*"

"They lost in overtime."

"No. I know that. Them's the only words George can say. *Did the Leafs win?*"

"Jesus. Did he have his stroke while he was watching the hockey game?"

"I guess." Edna hangs her cardigan carefully on the padded hanger. She knit it herself, so she's careful to keep it nice.

"Must've been Saturday, then."

"What?"

"That he had his stroke. Come to think of it, it was Saturday evening when the ambulance came. You called me away from Coach's Corner, remember?"

"Marie says to help yourself before the pickeroonies come. They'll show up as soon as it starts to get dark, she says. What do you want to bet that Harold Simms will be the first to arrive in that white van of his? Imagine what his house must look like? No wonder he's a bachelor."

Ralph stands and goes to the front hall. He crosses his arms over his barrel chest and looks out the diamond-shaped window in the door. "I don't guess I need an old toaster or a ten-speed bike," he says.

"There's a snow shovel out there. Looks new. I says to Marie, I says, are you sure you want to throw out that shovel? And she says, Lord, yes. We got six or seven, she says. How many snow shovels can a person use? I went, won't George be mad when he gets home? And Marie went, he won't be in much shape to argue, will he? What with he can only say four words now. So I says, I hope it don't give him another stroke when he sees all his stuff gone. And Marie says, this stuff has been giving me a stroke for years. Anyways. I told her you might come and get that snow shovel. It looks brand new."

"If I want a snow shovel, I'll go to Canadian Tire and buy a snow shovel."

"Marie says don't be surprised if we see Joe Anderson taking pictures of her house. She's putting it on the market. Wants to move into one of them condos down by the lake. No yard work she says."

"No garage either," says Ralph, sinking into the couch and pulling the afghan up over his big gut.

"That's right. No garage. And maybe no George either, if she's lucky."

"I thought you liked George."

"I like George fine, but I don't have to live with him, do I. You going to put the trash out?"

"Later. After my nap. If that's acceptable to you."

Edna fills the kettle and puts it on the front burner of the stove. Stray droplets sizzle angrily.

"The snow shovel's likely to be gone by then," Edna says. "That's all."

You Asked for It

Trish is ambitious. She graduated from teacher's college in the spring and she is on her way to her first assignment, a grade five class on an Anishinaabe reserve in northern Ontario. She expects to encounter issues. Poverty. Violence. Thanks to her dad's friends who work for the Ontario Provincial Police, she knows that there are about five hundred violent crimes each year. Stabbings mostly. Knives are the weapons of choice. But the good news is that it's been a long time since a teacher or a nurse has been hurt. Usually they just stab each other. So.

The population hovers around two thousand and a quarter of them are kids, enrolled at Peeneysee Eshkotay School. Enrolled, but not necessarily attending. Absenteeism is chronic, especially at the high school level. Many of the kids in grades ten to twelve are parents. The graduation rate is very, very low. Some years, there are no graduates at all. A successful year would see eight kids walking across the stage to get their high school diplomas, but the likelihood that any of them would go on to college or university is poor. None of this bothers Trish. She is confident that she can be successful with her class of ten-year-olds. She is generally a successful person. School, swim team, music. She knows how to set goals and achieve them.

At the airport in Red Lake, she has to switch planes. There are three rookie teachers waiting for the small plane that flies to the island every day. The pilot is a young boy in a hooded sweatshirt. He tells them they will have to carry their luggage on their laps and then he hops in the cockpit. Trish protests loudly and demands to see his license. At this point, a group of men, bent double with laughter, approach the plane and the real pilot presents himself. The kid glares at Trish and then barks out a nervous laugh.

On the plane ride the boy does not respond when Trish introduces herself and asks for his name. He smells. She knows there is no running water in ninety percent of the homes, but she didn't anticipate the odor of unwashed hair, dirty underwear, wood fire smoke. She learns very quickly to breathe through her mouth.

Peeneysee Eshkotay School is a collection of portable classrooms erected after the real school was burned to the ground. It was an accident. Three eight-year-old boys playing with matches in the supply room. There is no gym. No library. Trish spends a couple of days rounding up supplies like chart paper and notebooks and pencils. She sweeps and moves tables and decorates the bulletin board. Teaching has been her dream for a long time. She writes a big welcome sign in English and Ojibway and posts it on her door before she locks up and heads back to the trailer she shares with Monica, the high school art teacher. The sun has disappeared behind the black spruce and the pink glow in the sky is the first glimpse of beauty she has seen since she arrived. Counter to the impression of native culture she attained in Aboriginal Studies 101 at university, no one seems to give a shit about the environment here. Diapers and pizza boxes wash up on the beach like dead and bloated fish.

Two shadows emerge from the walkway between her portable and the one next door. They are boys, or men, with hoodies pulled over baseball caps. They shamble. That is the only word she can think of to describe the way they walk. Purposefully purposeless, they block her way. Even though she can see her trailer on the other side of the muddy playground, she has no illusions about how far a scream would travel. She knows that she is showing them fear and she imagines that they are amused by it.

"You got a cigarette, Miss?" the tall one asks.

"No," she says. "Sorry. I don't smoke." She makes a little sideways skip and waves as she walks away, trying to appear friendly, but they have already dismissed her and shambled on.

At school the next morning, she finds her welcome sign in the grass with a big dick drawn across it. Her heart starts racing. She tries not to take it personally. There is a short assembly in the sheltered area in front of the principal's portable. The principal is Mary, a rough-looking woman who waved goodbye to the backside of optimism a long time ago. This leadership position is the end of a long train wreck of a career sabotaged by bad luck and personal tragedies.

The first day in the classroom drags on. Minutes seem like hours. The kids do not talk. They do not respond to camp songs or picture books. They do not even answer roll call. Then Jordan arrives, the young *pilot*. He is late and high. He stands behind Trish and writes something on the blackboard in Ojibway and everyone laughs. They are suddenly out of control. She tries the PA system but it doesn't work. In desperation, she runs out the door and reports the chaos to the principal.

"Follow me," the principal says. In the classroom, the kids are sitting quietly at their desks. The blackboard has been erased.

"Don't make me call your dad," the principal tells Jordan.

After school, Trish puts on her running gear. She runs past the portables and the trailers and the nursing station. She runs past the OPP station where a high chain link fence topped with barbed wire protects the vulnerable officers. They are here on two-week stints earning extra points that they can exchange for vacation time or bonus bucks. Apparently the incidence of PTSD is too high if they stay longer. The violence is particularly gruesome in this community. Last week a guy stabbed his pregnant girlfriend in the stomach when he heard a rumor she'd been with someone else. It might not be his baby. Now it is nobody's baby.

The police cruiser pulls up alongside her. "Ma'am? Miss?"

Trish stops and pulls her earplugs out. "Yes? Hello."

"Maybe no one told you, but you shouldn't be out on your own. It's not a good idea. Maybe you can get a friend to run with you?"

"Sure. Sorry. I'm new."

"How was the first day of school?"

"It was hell, actually." The officers laugh.

"Welcome to Thunderbird First Nation," they say. "You be careful."

She waves and circles back toward town passing by The Northern, the only store on the reserve. It is run by an Indian family. Dot, not feather. They have groceries, lottery tickets, a Pizza Hut franchise and a KFC kiosk. They sell clothing and drug store items. But no alcohol. This is a dry band. But solvents and gasoline and pharmaceuticals are plentiful. When people get flown down to the hospital in Red Lake to have a baby or get treated for pneumonia, they always come back with oxycodone tucked away in their backpacks or sewn into the baby's sleepers.

Trish passes the beach. She is almost home when she sees a cluster of young people looking out across the water to the far shore, purple in the twilight. They seem to be gazing at something precious. Something Trish cannot see and never will. One girl turns around, her placid expression says, *we know you are there.* That is all. And Trish's heart races as if she has been threatened.

On Wednesday morning Trish arrives in her classroom determined to engage the kids and establish her authority. She has read some literature about classroom management and she is feeling confident after listening to her roommate's stories. "Everyone has some difficulty adjusting to a new culture," Monica says.

Trish gets off to a good start by reading a story about some kids who got lost in the bush. Her students are drawing maps as a follow up activity when Jordon saunters in. His hoodie is pulled up over his cap, cap pulled low. Hands in pockets. He nods at Trish as if he is the inspector here to evaluate her program. Jordan walks down one aisle and up the next. He is looking at the work the others are doing. He stops at Kandice's desk and watches for a while. He mumbles something to her. She does not respond or even look up. He takes a seat and opens his hands as if to say. Okay. I'm here. Where's my paper? Trish points to the supplies laid out on the craft table. Different kinds of paper, scissors, glue, coloured pencils. Jordan looks around at the other kids who are focusing intently on their tasks. And then he propels himself out of his chair, collects a few items, and comes toward the teacher's desk. He wants instructions, Trish thinks. As she turns to get the storybook about the lost kids, Jordan cuts off the tip of her braid. Snip. He shrugs at the class, shoves the hank of hair in his pocket and retreats to the back of the room.

Trish is in shock. She is utterly humiliated. With vertigo threatening to topple her at every step, she stumbles out the door and manages to find the principal's office before she dissolves in uncontrollable, choking, grief-stricken sobs. The principal, believing Trish has been assaulted, calls the nursing station and the police.

Trish wakes up, groggy and disoriented from the medication. The nurse on duty is young. Younger than her. She sits at Trish's bedside hugging her sweater to her.

"You okay?"

"Thirsty."

The girl goes and gets her a bottle of water and loosens the cap. She helps Trish get propped up with an extra pillow. Then she goes back inside her sweater and sits down.

"What happened?"

"This boy. In my class. He cut my hair. He grabbed my braid when I turned away from him and he cut the end off of it."

"That's it?"

"Yeah."

It is quiet except for a compressor or a generator or something. A machine breathing in and out that reminds her of her father snoring at the cottage where the walls do not go all the way to the ceiling. It makes her feel safe.

"Just that, not to minimize what you're feeling, but there's a lot worse. We see a lot worse."

Trish goes back to sleep and in the morning she has a shower and washes her hair. The nurse helps her even it out with a pair of bandage scissors.

"Do you ever get used to this place?"

"God, no. It's a hell hole. I'm paying off my student loan, then I'm outta here."

Trish is ready to go home. She walks over to the principal's office. Mary is talking on the phone with a cigarette dangling from her lip like a punk in an old movie. The lines in her face are the deep and permanent scars of hard living. Mary motions for her to take a chair. She offers Trish a cigarette and Trish accepts. This is a scene she didn't picture when she visualized her first week of teaching grade five.

"So," Mary says as she puts the phone back on the receiver, "Jordan seems quite taken with you."

"Excuse me?"

"Jordan. I went over to his house last night to have a chat with his dad. His big brother says that Jordan has a crush on you."

Trish feels sick. She slouches a bit in the chair and takes a drag. She has somehow attracted the misguided attentions of a ten year old boy and now . . . what? This is her fault? Like the Halloween Dance in high school when her boyfriend gave her a shove right in front of everybody. And then she ended up apologizing to him. "You were asking for it," he told her, crushing her close as the band played *Closing Time*.

"I didn't do anything to . . . "

"You didn't have to. You're cute and blonde and he thinks he loves you. That's all. I suspended him for three days. But he's here in the resource room with Troy. The special ed teacher. If we let him stay home for three days he'd just be getting high."

"Do you think I should quit? Resign? I feel like I should leave."

"No! Hell no. Let that kid get the best of you? Over my dead body. You'll be fine. Believe me. Now, you know, we don't have supply teachers here so your whole class is doubled up with Nancy's grade eights. She's a hard ass, so they'll be glad to see you back. I'll buzz over and let her know you're ready to pick them up?"

"I'm not. Not ready . . . " Trish looks at the clock. It is just about ten o'clock. "Tell them to come back after recess. Give me a chance to get my activity centres laid out."

"Atta girl. You'll toughen up. Drop in at lunch and let me know how it's going."

Trish did not see Jordan for two weeks. "He gone to the moose hunt with his uncle," Kandice had told her when she dared to enquire. Trish could count on Kandice and Kaylee. They were cute and clean and they wore identical wool hats with animal ears on them. They acted like normal teenyboppers with a whole repertoire of eye-rolling and mean girl gossip and giggling, but she could communicate with them. They were on her team. "They family gots a hunt camp on Rock Lake. His uncle is Chief. They rich."

Great. So now she has to worry about being on the Chief's radar. You don't want to piss off the Chief or the elders in this community. One thing she has learned, you never badmouth band council. The band pays your salary.

"You work for the band," Mary reminds them at the next staff meeting. "There is always the threat of getting BCR'd."

"What's --"

"Band Council Resolution. They come and get you and put you on a plane outta here."

On the second of October, with a heavy frost on the ground, Trish leaves her trailer and almost steps on a moose head. It is looking at her with cloudy eyes. A stray dog is sitting nearby with a questioning look, as if asking whether Trish is interested in eating it or not.

"Help yourself," Trish says.

The dog has been following her around and seems to have adopted Trish. She is a medium sized dog with a skittish personality and a triangular face like a fox. Trish has named her Vixen. Trish takes one more look at the moose head and braces herself for a challenging day. It looks like Jordan has left her a message. He is back.

Except Jordan doesn't show up. He is staying away from school. No big deal. Attendance fluctuates despite all the motivators in place, like pizza and gum and reward points for special events. The best the school can hope for on any given day is seventy percent of the school population arriving in the morning. Some just stay for breakfast and then leave. On a cold day, attendance might drop to as low as thirty percent. Sometimes, the teachers show up only to find that band council has cancelled school for the day. They announce cancellations in Ojibway on the radio station. Sometimes there is a reason, like problems with the power generator. Sometimes it is out of respect for a death in the community. If an elder dies, school might be closed for a week.

Trish does not see Jordan at all until one night, when her roommate is taking a first aid course at the Community Centre. She has a shower and wraps a towel around herself and goes out to sit by the stove where it is warm. She dries her hair and brushes it, leaning toward the heat. It is almost long enough to braid again, she thinks, and then she looks up and sees a face at the kitchen window. She locks herself in the bathroom and stays there until Monica gets home two hours later.

"Jordan was watching me," she tells Monica.

Monica thinks she might be imagining it. She goes outside and tries to hoist herself up to the kitchen window but it's too high.

"Maybe he got a boost," Trish says.

"Maybe he carries a ladder with him," Monica says.

"You don't believe me."

"Well, I think you might have seen a reflection. You know. Maybe an ATV was going by and caught the glass in a certain way."

"It was a face."

Trish starts to think she will make it to Christmas holidays. Her plan is to get home and then resign by email. There is no shame, she decides in quitting. She will say she has been offered another job. She has experience, now, for her résumé, and she will get herself on the supply-teaching list in her home community. She cannot wait to sleep in her childhood bedroom with the unicorn wallpaper. She hopes her mother hasn't changed it into a sewing room or an office like her friends' mothers have done with their old rooms.

The kids in her class are calmer now that the landscape has frozen solid. They like the Christmas activities she has organized for them. Colouring reindeer, letters to Santa, dot-to-dot candy canes. It is almost enough to make her think she could come back after the holidays and survive a whole year. At recess one day, when the temperature hovers around zero, she takes her tea outside and sits on the portable steps watching the kids play. Some of her students are in the field kicking at a snow bank. They have found something that was buried in the last storm. When they excavate it, they kick it back and forth. A ball. But it is not a ball. Trish is curious. She strolls over. Not close enough to interrupt the game, but near enough to see it is a puppy. A black puppy.

Back in her town, if children found a dead puppy on the school grounds, there would be a lockdown until the proper authorities arrived to take the body away and dispose of it. There would be grief counselors for the kids who found the puppy.

But here? No. A frozen, dead puppy is a ball or a puck. These kids are well acquainted with the real bogeyman. Death is a frequent and familiar visitor. Most of them have crosses in their front yards, marking the graves of brothers or aunts that have died young by suicide or overdoses or violence. Or freezing to death. Monica tells her the story. It happened last winter. The little boy who disappeared. Nine years old. No one saw him for five days and then finally, there was a mitten in a snow bank. And it had a hand in it. And the little boy's body was found, all bruised and broken. The coroner flew in from somewhere. Red Lake, probably. And he didn't even bother to investigate. Didn't stay overnight in the one motel where every single window is broken. Death by misadventure, the report indicated.

"The thing is, there was no amber alert. No news report. Even after he was found. Murdered. Nothing in the *Wawatay News* or the *Winnipeg Free Press* or the *Thunder Bay Chronicle*. I scoured them all."

"Why didn't you call the media?" Trish asks.

"Because. I would've got BCR'd. I know. It's wrong. But we're not going to fix it, you and me. This is what poverty looks like, Trish. No voice. No choice."

"So somebody gets away with murder?"

"Nobody gets away with anything here."

Trish worries that the dead dog will spread some kind of disease and marches to the office to report it. The secretary laughs. "The wolves will get it, love. It'll be gone in the morning."

Trish finishes the day by reading aloud from *Little House on the Prairie*. The kids like it. They like the challenges of pioneer life. The crop failures and the bad weather and way the Ingalls family makes do with very little. They like Pa and Ma, parents who fiddle after dinner and read Bible stories by the fire. Many of Trish's students go to the little Christian church on the north end of the island. The missionaries have been here for years. Decades. They are fundamentalists, and their mission is funded by some organization in Kentucky. Biblical graffiti is a formidable rival for swear words on public buildings. Someone has spray-painted a warning on the back door of the Community Centre. *Suicide is a mortal sin, a grave offence to God who gives life and reserves the right to take it away.* The cemetery behind the church has a snow fence around it. No suicides allowed.

In the dark days of December, the sun sets before the end of the school day. Trish locks her classroom and heads over to the Community Centre where it is bright and full of people there for bingo night. Cigarette smoke hangs like a storm cloud in the stratosphere below the florescent lights. After playing two games, she gives her sheets and her dauber to Abby King, the thirty-two year old grandmother sitting next to her, and begs off with a headache.

The night is still. A full moon lights up the shabby landscape. Vixen comes running out of the cardboard box on her porch where Trish stuffed some old quilts she found at the dump. Good. She hasn't been around for a while and Trish was starting to worry. "Hey girl. Hey, sweet girl. You want a treat? You hungry?"

Trish is surprised to see the lights on in her trailer. Monica was supposed to be at the church tonight, helping with the Christmas Concert rehearsal. The door is unlocked. Even before she notices the mess, Trish gets a whiff of the sickening smell. The feral smell of a power imbalance that no amount of air freshener can cover up.

The fridge is open and all the condiments are smashed on the kitchen floor or dumped on the couch. Mice scurry as she screams and slams the door. She vomits over the porch railing and then starts walking in the direction of the church.

Monica is so practical and reassuring. "Kids," she says. "It was the last day for the high school kids before the holidays and they were raising a little hell, that's all. No damage done. Ketchup stains on the couch. Mustard stains on the rug. No big deal."

But it is a big deal. Monica cleaned it up, but she saw it. The word cunt spelled out in barbeque sauce on her mirror. She knows who did this. She just knows.

Trish starts worrying about next week. Monica is getting a flight out after the concert. The high school teachers are done, but she has to stay on until next Wednesday when the elementary teachers finish up. So. She will sleep in the nursing station. Or bunk in with the married couple who have the trailer closest to the OPP station. She will be fine.

Sunshine makes a big difference. Reflecting off the snow, it sparkles and lightens everyone's mood. There are festivities. The Christmas cookie exchange and the concert and Craft Night. There is a vague sense of hope and excitement when the Director of Education dresses as Santa and delivers chocolate bars to each class. The Director is twenty-four years old, the nephew of the Chief. A high school grad. A nice young man. But what he doesn't know about running a board of education is a lot. He has a blog on the school's website and recently he wrote about the hockey tournament in Dog Lake where he did some "crotch watching". Trish is horrified, but Monica thinks it's funny. "He means well," she said. "It's not his fault he has no guidance."

With all the good cheer, Trish relaxes and hugs Monica good-bye. Her first evening alone goes well enough. Trish does some beading on a leather key chain that she is making for her sister. She listens to the radio, mostly Christmas carols. At nine thirty, she gets in her pajamas and pulls on her siwash sweater and climbs into bed. She leaves the bathroom light on and the light over the stove too. Before she locks up, Trish steps out onto the porch and checks to see that Vixen is in her shelter. The dog responds with a quiet whimper and a quick wag of her tail. Trish longs to bring the dog inside, but that is taboo in this community. Dogs are wild. People would think she was crazy.

Trish falls asleep reading her book. It is not even midnight when a full-blown panic attack wakens her. She cannot move, immobilized as if the Nazis are walking on floorboards inches above her head. Prickly with pins and needles, she tries to breathe. She hears the fridge kick in. She feels someone sitting at the foot of the bed. Some primal sound escapes from deep in her heart and the dog barks on the porch. Trish is propelled up and out from under the covers and finds herself under the clear cold constellations. Her wool socks are sticking to the ice. Vixen is alert and worried.

The night is endlessly quiet. Rationality tells Trish that she had a night terror. They are worse than nightmares because they feel so real. The bed rolls and heaves. A conspiracy of shadowy evil-doers has arranged to have you sucked into another dimension. Death is imminent. Trish sits on the bottom step of the little porch and lets the dog put her head in her lap.

What are the chances that a ten-year-old boy is sitting on the end of her bed? Few to none.

Trish wishes her self-talk was more convincing. She wishes she had grabbed a knife. Her bum is starting to freeze and her flannel pajamas stick to the icy step as she attempts to stand. She needs to get back inside before she gets a chill but the door won't open. It is locked. Someone has turned the deadbolt. From the inside.

Trish grabs the quilt out of the dog's bed and wraps it around her shoulders. She jogs across the open field, her wool socks gathering clots of snow until she slips and lands hard on her right knee. Rolling onto her side, she pushes herself upright on her good leg and limps along with gritted teeth past the empty school portables toward the blue light of the police station. And then she realizes she's alone.

"Vixen?"

"Vixen!"

"No . . . "

The northern lights creep along the horizon and reflect on the snow, creating the illusion of oceanic swells. Ancient waves of aqua and teal move relentlessly over the cold town, obliterating small struggles.

Grim Things

The group meets every day for coffee and the breakfast special. They sit at the long community table and welcome anyone who wants the benefit of their shared wisdom. I know how they like their eggs, how crispy they like their bacon, whether they prefer rye toast or whole wheat. They tip good.

These are men who are not shy about expressing their opinions. They are not in favour of bringing in Muslims or refugees from Syria and they don't tone it down when the gas station owner joins them. They call him Rog instead of Raj and he takes their prejudice with the good humour one allows the unworldly. Raj has shifted their thinking about brown people, although they do not realize it. They see how he works hard and volunteers at the fire hall. They notice that his kids win all the awards at the school. He has more kids than anybody else in town, and they tell him he is singlehandedly keeping the high school open. The enrolment is half what it was when their kids went there.

This group has been around a long time. There is Larry, the real estate agent, nicknamed "The King" because of his pronouncements that are hard to argue with. Bob owns the car dealership and his nickname is Billy. Not sure why. There is a chartered accountant and a banker and a lawyer and a bunch of business owners. Then there are the retired guys who roll in just as the working fellows are heading to their jobs, about nine o'clock. The comings and goings continue all the way to lunch if the special looks good.

Some of them bring the local paper in to read the obits and look at who's got their picture in this week. They shake their heads at the town hall report and wonder what happened to all the men. The women on council are either lesbians or *not that smart.* There hasn't been a lady Reeve elected yet. There are two in the county now, but not in this township.

For the most part, these men are respectful and polite. They call me by name and remember to ask after my mother, who is in Extendicare, and my son, who is in my basement. "Verna," they say. "How's Jason doing?" They all have family members who are disappointments. They all have struggles, for sure.

By listening to their gossip for the better part of ten years, I have learned more than I want to know about this bunch. Their children, with the exception of a few, have messed up big time. Divorces, DUI's and bankruptcies. Their grandkids are on drugs, glued to their phones, tattooed, lazy and rude. How did things get so bad? The theories are endless. They laugh a lot. You've got to look for the humour in grim things.

Like suicide. There are quite a few of them nowadays. Suicide has been around for a long time, but back in the day, it was not reported. *Hush, hush.* They can tell you a dozen stories about men who ended the pain with a twelve gauge. It is not such a bad way to go if you do it out behind the barn. Mostly, it works out as intended, but the odd time it don't.

Like there is Half Head for example, who comes in for coffee with his daughter once or twice a week. He blew out the top corner of his head. Old Doc McCrae said it was the neatest lobotomy he ever seen. And it worked, too. Fred's been as happy as a pig in shit ever since. He's forgot all about his bad debts and the wife leaving town.

Hanging. Now that's more gruesome. Somebody has to cut you down. And the car running in the shed is a nasty thing to come upon, like the Saunders kid who opened the garage door to get his bike out and found his dad all turned blue. They all agree that a gun works best. Aimed right, it's the best way. But most of them will end up where my mother is, languishing in a long-term care bed, moaning about some worry that don't exist anymore.

They call themselves the Liar's Club. I thought it was unique until I went to Nova Scotia and saw a bench out front of some small town Legion with the same name carved right into it. So, I guess there are Liar's Clubs right across the country. If you haven't heard some good gossip by ten o'clock, The King says, well, it's time to make something up. They speculate about the government, and what a waste of skin most government workers are. Like the two men who arrived in town last October from the Cemeteries Regulation Unit, Government of Ontario.

So these lads show up in suits. One oriental lad and one black as a boot. They are driving a rented sedan. They stay over two nights at the Red Pine Lodge, the most expensive accommodation available in the county. Separate rooms, in case you were wondering. Jack Armstrong's daughter works on the front desk so she can attest to that. With all the gays around now, you never can tell.

These lads are inspecting the little country cemeteries that are not owned and operated by the municipality. Like the little graveyard behind Canfield United. It is old. There are a bunch of pioneer graves that are hard to read. But people still get interred at Canfield to be alongside family.

An honorarium of nine hundred dollars a year goes to the person who is in charge of upkeep. Now here is the part that chafes. These city fellas have come to check the accounting books of poor old Bev Reiner who has kept up the graveyard for the past twenty some years. He has cut the grass and shoveled the snow and arranged to have the fresh graves dug. He has repaired the fences and put new gravel on the pathway so the mourners don't get muddy. He has done all that at his own personal loss. The nine hundred bucks hasn't never come close to covering all the expenses. But one thing Bev was not good at and that was writing things down. He has a shoe box of random receipts but it's hard to tell what all they are for. Bev has always paid Gordie Williams in cash to bring his ditch witch in to dig the graves. And when he's been suffering with arthritis too bad to cut the grass himself, he has paid the young Sedore lad twenty bucks out of his own pocket. He righted all the old pioneer graves after that bad storm flooded the back corner. Built boxes and filled them with cement and got those headstones standing straighter than they had in a hundred years. Took him a few months. Old Pork Wilkinson helped him. They did it the old way, one bag of cement at a time, mixing the stuff up in the wheelbarrow and smoothing it with a straight piece of lumber.

The Government, though, has some rules about how their nine hundred dollars is spent. Apparently, there are forms to be filed and a whole lot of red tape. Permission to make improvements, like the fence and the pathway, was never granted. Those city boys had old Bev in tears, thinking he was going to jail over all the infractions he had made in his stupidity. Well, Bev's wife put in a phone call to The King who left his office in the middle of a transaction and drove out to Canfield and tore a strip off of those officials.

"Your goddamned hotel rooms cost more than this man's allotment," he says. "You should be ashamed of yourselves. The two of you make more in one day than this man makes in a year, and you want him to account for it? You want him to spend another ten or twenty hours a week filling in forms? If I sent you a bill for the number of hours this man has spent taking care of this here cemetery, it would cost you hundreds of thousands of dollars. Get your foreign asses in that car and get out of my town."

And they did. The only consequence was that Bev received a notice that the cemetery was officially closed. No more dead people. But Darlene Bishop applied for a grant to make the graveyard an official heritage sight and she got forty-eight thousand dollars to keep it endowed. Her committee gave an amount to Bev, in gratitude for services rendered, and offered him free graves for him and his wife when the time comes. They will back-date the interment so that the Government will never find out that fresh bodies were allowed in the gate after closing.

Grim things are less grim when you get a little win like that.

The Liar's Club got a lot of mileage out of that story. How The King sent those Government lads packing. It is still a favourite one to tell, even now that The King is down in the city getting chemo treatments for the cancer. They all wish they could go visit him in hospital but most of them don't drive no more and the ones that do, well they don't drive to the city. So. When he gets back there will be some stories about nurses and the medical system. We're all looking forward to it.

Blue Finger

Joyce is alone when it happens. It's like a bee sting in her baby finger. There is a small blue bruise as if she hammered it or slammed a drawer on it. But she hasn't done anything to cause trauma. Joyce feels a panicky worry erupting in her chest and wonders if there are blood vessels popping throughout her body. She goes to the front hall and looks in the mirror and smiles to see if one side of her face is drooping. It is not. The smile is even. But in the harsh overhead light, her reflection grins back at her. Sardonic.

Scornfully or cynically mocking. That was the definition of sardonic that she and her sisters read in the big Webster dictionary after watching Mr. Sardonicus on *The Late, Late Show*. Saturday's late night movie feature, usually a horror, was a regular pajama party event in the days before Netflix or VCRs.

Mr. Sardonicus, after digging up his father's grave to retrieve a winning lottery ticket, found the body to be grinning. Sardonically. And when he returned home, his own face was frozen in a sardonic smile. The condition was permanent. Sardonic. This word was tucked away with a small collection of treasures that Joyce kept hidden in her meager vocabulary, retrieving it occasionally like a miser who pulls out the dusty box of coins from under his bed to covet in secret.

Those halogen light bulbs Bert purchased will have to go. No one looks good in bright white light, but Joyce is alarmed at her haggard reflection. Her makeup is crumbly around her nose, like a mask made out of deteriorating latex. Her eyebrows are high and black above the pale blond ridges that she plucks. Her lipstick is bleeding into the tiny lines around her mouth. She looks like an alcoholic, which she was, has been. Is. She looks like a smoker, which she was, has been. Is still, occasionally.

The blue dot on the pad of Joyce's baby finger is still there, and now the area is numb. She feels afraid. Her husband is in the hospital. He is recovering from heart surgery. Bert is Joyce's third husband. He is controlling. Not in a mean way like her first two husbands, the pervert and the pyro. But in a way that makes her anxious when she is alone. If Bert were here he would tell her to take an aspirin and go to bed. "It's nothing," he would say. Or maybe he would put her in the car and drive her to Emerg. Joyce doesn't drive. Anymore. Either way, she wouldn't have to wonder or think or worry. She outsourced her decision-making to men years ago.

Joyce dials her oldest sister's number. She has five sisters. All pretty and fit, even in their fifties and sixties. Lena will tell her what to do. Sure enough, Lena checks Dr. Google and tells her she has Blue Finger. Common in middle-aged women. Often happens while doing regular activities like washing the dishes. And the blue area will spread a bit. By morning, your whole finger might be blue. But it will be gone in a few days. It's not connected to heart or stroke issues. Not to worry.

As a child, Joyce was always amazed how easy everything seemed to be for her big sister. Lena took everything in stride. Her joy was infectious. One day, Lena ran into the den and jumped on their father's lap. He was reclined in the easy chair, watching the news.

"Daddy," Lena said in a babyish voice. "I'm collecting money for a fundraiser at school. To build a school in Biafra."

Daddy pulled out a five-dollar bill and handed it over. "Is that enough?" he asked.

"Yes, Daddy. Thanks. You're the best, most generous Daddy in town." She kissed him on his scruffy cheek. He was a hairy man and his six o'clock shadow was fierce. Joyce would never have let herself get that close to the gruff old bear that was her father. She was fascinated and horrified by her sister's performance.

Lena hopped up and walked past Joyce who was sitting primly at the dining room table working out some impossible algorithm. Lena stuffed the bill in her jeans pocket, grabbed the pencil out of Joyce's hand, and solved the problem in twenty seconds.

"There ya go, Mouse," she said.

Joyce's heart is calming down. She creeps into bed and sucks her blue finger for a while like a pacifier and worries about Bert. She wants him to get completely better, the way he was before the heart attack, or die. She does not want him to be an invalid. If she has to help him shower or get dressed, she will go crazy.

Joyce married her first husband when she was still a kid. In those days, when you got in *trouble* you married the father or killed yourself. Joyce never for a second blamed Kent for her situation. She was grateful that he did the right thing. While Kent got his degree at the university, Joyce did farm work and the farmers let them live in a trailer by the cornfield. She picked and baled and milked and shoveled manure. The baby was a quiet little girl named Beth who toddled around the barn contentedly.

The farmers, Ev and Jim, were good to her. One day, Jim pulled up a chair while she was milking.

"Me 'n Ev. We're gonna have to ask your husband to leave," he said.

Joyce's heart was pounding and her face got all flushed. She knew what he was talking about.

"Kent's been seen around town," Jim told her, "doing things that a Christian man wouldn't do. And Ev caught him flashing the Mennonite ladies behind the baler."

Joyce felt sick, sick, sick. Kent had this need to show himself in public. It wasn't his fault. His parents were nuts.

"You don't have to go with him," Jim said kindly. He was looking at his hands. His voice was barely a whisper. "It's your choice, of course, but you and the baby are welcome to stay on with us as long as you want. Life won't likely be easy for you either way. But, we think you might be better off. On your own."

That night, Jim and two of the migrant workers drove Kent to the bus station. Joyce knew he didn't really love her, but she thought he would've put up a fight for her and Beth. That all happened in June and by Thanksgiving the papers were signed and she was divorced.

Joyce met Dick, a neighbouring farmer, at Jim and Ev's church. Dick was a big Dutch man, ten years older than Joyce, with a lot of rules about housework and wifely duties. This suited Joyce fine. She liked rules. Which was funny in a way, because she hated rules when she was growing up. No one was allowed to open the fridge door except her parents. And curfew? Joyce's mother put a Big Ben alarm clock just inside the front door set for 11 p.m. and if you got in under the wire, you turned the alarm off. If you were even one minute late, the alarm would sound and her father would be sitting, arms crossed, in his lazy boy chair with details about how long you were grounded. *God help you* if you turned the alarm off for a tardy sister. Somehow her parents always knew.

By the time Joyce was twenty-five, she and Dick had two kids of their own. For some reason, her husband had taken a real dislike to Beth. According to him, she was spoiled and stubborn and likely to turn out rotten like her father.

"Send her back to her real dad," Dick told her.

And she did. Joyce was exhausted trying to intervene between Beth and her stepfather. She thought it would be better for everyone. But the years after Beth left were not better. Dick was brooding and suspicious. He worried that Joyce might tell their business to Ev and Jim and the other busybodies at the church. They stopped going to services.

Dick burned things. It started with a rusty barrel out the back for burning junk mail. Cardboard. Packaging. He seemed to get great pleasure out of fire. One day, the shed burned to the ground. Then the hen house. He experimented with accelerants. Joyce started to sleep with one eye open. She was convinced that Dick was going to burn her alive and cash in on the insurance policy.

Occasionally, when she had the opportunity to get to the mailbox before Dick, Joyce found correspondence from the Netherlands. She could not read Dutch, but the handwriting was feminine. Maybe he left a wife in Amsterdam when he emigrated.

Maybe he had Dutch children. It was clearly none of her business. Dick never told her anything, except that she was stupid.

Joyce thinks it odd that her name sounds carefree and happy. Something is missing in her, emotionally, and she can't fake it. Her mother and father and sisters all like each other and hug when they meet at Christmas and Walker family reunions. They have tons of cousins and friends and commitments. Sports and community stuff. They are always raising money for some kid with cancer or buying a wheelchair for an old army vet.

Shortly after the kids moved away, Joyce worked in Ladies Lingerie at Sears. Every morning, she arrived at work, having taken great care with her hair and makeup and clothes. Joyce loved punching in, putting her card into the machine and knowing that her work would be recognized with a real paycheque. She was good with the customers, especially hard to serve clients who were difficult to fit or simply difficult to please. After a year, Joyce was recommended for a management position. She was reliable and efficient. A top sales associate. But Dick didn't appreciate her success.

"It costs half your income just to operate a vehicle," he said. "Gas is getting expensive. And besides, I need you on the farm."

Trapped out on King Road all winter with no car, Joyce caught pneumonia and lost weight. She couldn't warm up, not even inside, because Dick wouldn't pay for the heat to be cranked up when "nobody" was home. If he caught her in the house making coffee or watching Oprah, there was payment due. He wore her down. It was him or her, she realized and she had to do something to get herself off the damn farm. One gloomy February day, the wind was howling down the chimney and she ached all over. She needed to stay in bed. Dick told her if she wasn't in the barn when he got back from town with cigarettes, he'd kick her ass. When he drove up the laneway an hour later, the farmhouse was burning.

The Walkers were wonderful in a tragedy. Lena held a fund-raiser to get Joyce back on her feet. Then she helped Joyce find a little apartment in Toronto. The family wanted her nearby so they could keep an eye on her. Her health was not good.

Dick went to jail. The Fire Marshall had been thorough.

One thing about Joyce, though, she was never long without a man. She managed to hook up with Bert three weeks after her arrival in the city. He was a bachelor, the building superintendent. His mother had recently moved into a long-term care facility after some embarrassing incidents with the master keys. Joyce went with Bert to visit the mother who cried and begged to come home and then screamed at him that she wished he'd never been born.

Joyce took over the visits to Bert's mother while Bert saw to the building. Plumbing, electrical, drywall repairs. Bert was quite handy, but he didn't work fast. "I'd rather fix it right the first time," he said.

Joyce was thrifty. She was a good cook. And she didn't expect to be cuddled or coddled like other women he had tried dating in the past. In fact she was fine if they didn't have sex at all.

"Surprise!" Joyce announced to the Walker clan at her parents' fiftieth anniversary party. "Bert and I are getting married."

Until the heart attack, it was working out pretty well. But now Joyce was lost. She did not want the responsibility of leaky faucets and plugged toilets. "You'll have to fix it yourself," she told everyone who phoned with a complaint. "My husband is in the hospital."

The owner of the building had been by twice. She looked through the peephole and didn't let on that she was home. Finally he sent a letter with a "termination of employment". He would hire an interim caretaker for six weeks while the couple found a new place to live.

Lena could have done the work with one hand tied behind her back. Vacuuming, lawn care, shoveling snow. But Joyce did not have the stamina.

The Blue Finger went away. By the time Bert was released, there was no trace of that tiny aberration that had frightened her so. He lay beside her now, solid and self-assured. His heart was like a bear's heart, the doctor told him. Bert made an agreement with the owner to extend the caretaker's duties. He would do the light work and gradually take over the heavier tasks. He never asked Joyce to pitch in. She went to exercise class and watched her soaps and visited Bert's mother. She made meals with low cholesterol, switching up her soup recipes with broth instead of cream. It was all she could manage, and Bert was fine with that. He never expected more.

After Lena got the five dollars from their dad, Joyce watched as she grabbed her coat and skipped out the door. She came back with a pack of KOOL's menthol. Lena and their middle sister, Gwen scurried behind the garden shed to light one up. They passed it back and forth. When they saw Joyce standing there, looking so serious, they both laughed and offered her a drag.

She didn't sleep that night. In the morning, she followed her dad out to the driveway. He rolled down the window.

"What's up, Mouse?"

"Daddy," she said. "Lena bought cigarettes with the Biafra money you gave her."

Her father looked at her. That disappointed look. He took a deep breath.

"You need to learn something about loyalty, Mouse. Lena would never tattle on you. A tattletale ends up with no friends. Now, off you go and get ready for school."

Joyce feels the vibrations of the expressway buzzing up through the foundation of the building and coursing through her body. Suddenly, a sharp pain in her finger sends her rushing to the bathroom, dizzy and panicky. She manages to close the door behind her before she turns on the light. It is nothing. No Blue Finger. She is fine. She lowers the toilet seat and sits down and takes deep breaths until she is able to find the vodka bottle under the sink. It is 2 a.m. and she is tempted to call Lena, just to test her loyalty.

Dick never contacted her. Even after he got out of jail, he didn't track her down and kill her as she thought he might. He was a coward after all. And now he is an old man. She climbs back between the covers and spoons up against Bert's boney back, pressing against him until she feels the big bear heart beating. She smiles, sardonically, and falls fast asleep.

The Exhibition

Jane and Cynthia were inseparable. They both lived in palatial brick homes sheltered by shade trees on Lochlin's wide main street. Their daddies were rich.

Jane lived at 400 Broad Street. Her daddy owned the Monarch Knitting Factory on River Street. Ralph Randle was an imposingly big man who wore a well-cut suit to work. He was a respected boss, known to be sympathetic, especially during the war years when the big machines were run by women. Sweaty and covered with lint, they surprised him with their ability to do a man's job. And they were reliable, too. Folks had warned him that the women would call in sick every time one of their kids had a sore throat, but that didn't happen. Productivity went up and stayed up. Ralph had a soft spot for his girls, as he fondly called them, especially big-breasted blondes who were sometimes given opportunities for training in bookkeeping or shorthand or typing. Office work. Although he took pride in the fact that his wife, Olivia, was educated and refined, Ralph found that he also had an appetite for foul-mouthed, coarse women who smoked cigarettes during their breaks.

Ralph had two children. He would have liked more but Olivia was opposed to it. There was Robert, popular among his peers for sarcastic comments about the high school teachers, and lovely Jane, whose thick red ringlets were mourned throughout the town when, on her twelfth birthday, she convinced her mother to let her go to the beauty parlor for a stylish bob.

Jane was clever at playing Daddy's girl when it suited her, though generally she was an undemanding child. She knew enough to appear at the dinner table with impeccable manners and a clean, freshly starched midi. She knew how to turn the mundane events of a day at school into delightful stories of spelling bees and British Bulldog games. She brought her art projects and handwriting notebook (with stamped stars at the top of every page) to the supper table for the praise her father bestowed.

Not that she was vain, as Robert assumed (far be it from him to brag about his school work), it was just that she knew it made her father happy. As long as she could remember, Jane understood that it was her job to keep him happy. Jane often thought how little effort it took. It was as simple as asking for his advice. When she needed his help with her pioneer project, his heart almost burst. Jane was Daddy's girl, all right.

The town counted on the whistle at the Monarch Knitting Factory to start the working day at eight, announce lunch at noon, and to signal quitting time at six. When the war ended, not willing to lose his female workforce, Ralph added two shifts. The afternoon shift went from four until twelve. The graveyard shift started at midnight and finished at eight in the morning. Mostly foreigners worked midnights; Italians and Dutch and even a few Germans who were bold enough to emigrate after all the grief Hitler had caused everybody.

Having three shifts meant that the women who got used to a paycheque during the war years could keep right on working if they chose, and many did. Especially those whose sweethearts had been killed or worse, stolen by snooty English war brides. Some ambitious young married couples that wanted to buy a house and a car never saw each other. The wife would work days and give her husband a quick peck on the cheek as she passed him at the factory gate at four o'clock. Ralph even provided the service of company buses to attract workers from the poor communities down-river where the family farm was fast going out of style. He was clever, Ralph Randle.

Cynthia lived at 334 Broad Street. Her daddy was Gordon Craig, the pharmacist. Gordon had a good working relationship with the doctors in town. Craig Pharmacy was adjacent to the medical centre, a modern clinic where the seats in the waiting room were always full.

The increased availability of new medications and life-saving vaccinations made Gordon Craig rich. He was well respected by the doctors, especially since it was his caution about the drug thalidomide that kept the number of birth defects in Lochlin to a minimum. He took his responsibility to the community very seriously and spent his evenings pouring over medical journals and pharmaceutical material, tuning out his five children with amazing concentration.

Gordon golfed with the young doctors on Wednesday afternoons and when they organized a Kinsmen Club, he was asked to be on the first executive committee. In the town of Lochlin, Gordon Craig was considered to have integrity. He was trusted. He was, indeed, a big fish in a little town.

Cynthia was the second youngest of five Craig children. She had two older brothers, Jimmy and Bobby, and an older sister, Lorna (whom she despised). Her baby sister, Daisy, was a mongoloid with a great lolling tongue and, according to the whispered conversations of her aunts, would never read nor write and would not live past twenty. Cynthia's mother, Gwen, was sometimes criticized for refusing to put Daisy in the Riddell Home for the Retarded in Hamilton.

"You're wearing yourself out, Gwen, with the care of that one," Aunt Sally would tell her. "Think of the other children. You have no energy left over for them."

"It would be different if Gordon would hire some help for you," Aunt Kathleen added. "I know he's dead set against a housekeeper, but a cleaning lady once a week only costs five dollars. Even the Leaches have a cleaning lady, so they do. And Jim Leach is a *factory worker*. So he is."

"You know it's not the money, Kathleen," Gwen replied patiently, time and again. "Gordon feels that it's the children's responsibility to help with the chores. It builds character."

"It builds dirt and grime, more like it," Sally whispered to Kathleen while Gwen pulled fresh muffins out of the oven. Kathleen sniffed in agreement.

Cynthia secretly hated the aunts (the old maids, as her father called them) but her mother seemed to laugh them off.

"They're harmless," she said. "Women take housekeeping far too seriously these days. It's not important in the least. Why make extra work for yourself when it just gets messy again?"

The carpet in the sunroom, newly converted to the television room, was covered with an assortment of socks and sweaters and homework. In the living room, which most women kept as a pristine retreat for guests, there was always a half-finished jig-saw puzzle on the coffee table: a chateau in the Alps, or fishing boats in Peggy's Cove. Gwen preferred to seat company at the sticky yellow kitchen table, close to the coffee pot. That's the way her mother did it in the old farm kitchen, and none of her friends complained.

Instead of cleaning, Gwen went to the boys' football and bas-ketball games to cheer them on. She signed Lorna and Cynthia up for figure skating and sat in the cold arena with a runny-nosed, well-bundled Daisy, admiring figure eights and bunny hops. She drove the bunch of them out to Sandy Bay at the lake in her wood-paneled station wagon for Red Cross swimming lessons each July. They all had badges. Even Daisy, by the time she was eight, could float on her back and do a successful jellyfish, earning her a Tadpole Badge.

Gwen was popular with the other women who sat and cheered on their children. She was not stuck-up, as some women were when they married well. She was still Gwennie Clark, local girl, who had a kind word for everyone. She eschewed make-up and bought her clothes downtown at Helen's Dress Shop instead of trekking to the city like some. Her children were equally pop-ular; easy-going, athletic boys, and saucy, self-effacing Lorna, and Daisy, whose joyful presence in the community changed many attitudes about institutionalization. Only Cynthia, with her pinched expression and judgmental eyes, was unpopular. Sometimes Gwen shook her head as she observed Cynthia, so much like Sally and Kathleen in attitude and appearance. Thank goodness that Jane Randle had the patience to be her friend. Although, Gwen knew, Jane had many friends and Cynthia had but one.

Bullied by Lorna and ignored by her brothers, Cynthia loved to go to Jane's house. It was elegant and tidy. Everything had its place. Towels were folded just so on the warm rods in the bathrooms. Sheets were white and clean and smelled of Ivory Snow. There was always Pears Soap in the soap dish and toilet paper on the roll. The fridge was full of fresh fruit and petit fours and dainty sandwiches on coloured bread, leftovers from Mrs. Randle's entertaining.

The Randles did not socialize in the same circle as the Craigs. Olivia's friends were golfers and tennis players. They were educated. Olivia belonged to the University Women's Club and hosted the annual book drive, having studied English literature at the University of Toronto. She managed to sidestep conversations about Ralph's lack of a degree. He had attended Western for one year, but when his father became ill, he returned to run the factory. Ralph was secretly relieved. A Lochlin boy through and through, he did not embrace the town snobs as his peers. He was more comfortable at the local beer parlor or the ballpark. Ralph suffered through Olivia's "soirees" and missed her hoity-toity events as often as possible. He joined the Lions Club and the Rotary Club and the Masonic Lodge. Not that he attended all the meetings, but they gave him enough excuses to cover just about every night of the week if he needed them.

Just as Cynthia loved the quiet order of the Randle home, Jane loved the comfortable chaos of the Craig home. As soon as she dropped her sweater in a heap at the front door and kicked her shoes into the ever-present pile, she felt right at home. She'd pet the big golden retriever and give Daisy a hug. She traded comic books with Cynthia's brothers. She even appreciated the cleverness of Lorna's caustic remarks.

Jane took her friendship with Cynthia very much for granted. She liked Cynthia well enough, but she did not share her singular devotion. Jane had other friends. In fact, she had quite a following at school. She went to the Catholic Church Camp, a place that Cynthia, from a United Church family, could not follow. Jane was a Girl Guide. She took piano lessons. She belonged to a group of Highland Dancers. She fit in wherever she went.

Cynthia, on the other hand, avoided group activities. Unless her mother signed her up for something, like the dreaded figure skating at which she was abysmal, Cynthia kept her own council. Jealous as she was of Jane's other friends, she convinced herself that she was Jane's best friend, just as Jane was hers. And Jane never let on otherwise.

Cynthia kept track of every favour Jane bestowed upon her, religiously recording it in her locked diary. Every time Jane let Cynthia go first in skipping, lent her a sweater or gave her a compliment, it went into the diary. Cynthia felt that she could never repay Jane's generosity. She tried. Months before Jane's birthday, Cynthia would rack her brains for a memorable birthday present, but Jane, on frequent trips to the city, always managed to get a better, more expensive, more important gift.

In March when Jane turned twelve, she bobbed her hair. Cynthia, feeling like the husband in the story, *Gift of the Magi*, sadly returned the silver hair clips to the jewelry store and replaced them with a charm for Jane's bracelet. A pair of scissors. It was a terrific hit and got a big laugh around the Randle supper table where Cynthia was one of twenty guests. But in June, when Cynthia celebrated her twelfth birthday with a quiet family dinner, Jane gave her the perfect gift, an ID bracelet with her name engraved on the front, and FF on the back.

"It means friends forever," Jane whispered into her ear.

It broke Cynthia's heart that she hadn't thought of it first.

So, when Gordon Craig told Cynthia that he was treating the family to a day at the Canadian National Exhibition in Toronto at the end of August, she knew she had a wonderful way to repay her friend.

"May I bring Jane, Daddy?" she asked.

Gordon seldom noticed his twelve-year-old daughter these days. She was quiet. A reader. Her tentative voice was often lost among the rambunctious activities of her older siblings. How earnest she was, he noted.

"Of course, sweetie," he said, happy to see a rare smile on her face.

Cynthia could not wait until the next day. She raced up the street to tell Jane. They were going to the CNE. They were going to have a ball! They poured over the map of the Exhibition grounds that had been printed in the local newspaper and memorized all the midway rides. They decided to save the Flyer, billed as the best roller coaster in the world, for last.

The day before they were to go, Olivia Randle called Gwen Craig. Though they lived on the same street, they did not see each other frequently.

"What should Jane wear to the CNE?"

"Pardon?"

"The girls have been so excited, Gwen. Really, it's awfully kind of you to invite her. What is Cynthia going to wear tomorrow?"

"I don't understand, Olivia. Honestly, this is the first I've heard about it. If Cynthia invited Jane I . . . well I'm awfully sorry but, I don't see how I could manage taking an extra child along."

Gordon, listening to his wife's half of the conversation felt his stomach drop. He remembered promising Cynthia she could bring Jane. Of course he had expected her to clear it with Gwen. He had not, in fact, given it another thought.

"I must have a word with you," he whispered to Gwen. "It's my fault."

"May I call you right back, Olivia? I have a pot boiling over."

Gwen turned terrible glaring eyes toward her husband.

"What have you done, Gordon? It's quite impossible to take any other children to the CNE. I don't want the responsibility. Jane is Ralph Randle's little princess. If anything happened to her . . ."

"Relax, Gwen. Cynthia never asks me for anything. She asked weeks ago and I said yes."

"Well you had better un-say it. You'll have to tell her you made a mistake. You weren't thinking. There's hardly room enough in the car for our kids, even with Daisy staying at the farm with my sisters."

"She wouldn't take up much room, Gwen. The girl is reed-thin. Won't you reconsider? Please? I feel terrible. What will the Randles think of us?"

"You should be more concerned with what I think of you, Gordon. And right now, it's not much. If the Randles want Jane to go, they can take her themselves. It wouldn't kill Olivia to take a day away from her golf and tennis cronies. I'm sure they'd survive. And you know what Lorna would say if she knew Jane was coming. She'd have an absolute conniption. Believe you me, life would be miserable all the way to Toronto."

"They could ride in the back of the wagon..."

"No. This is meant to be a holiday for me, too, Gordon. I'll not take on the responsibility. I won't."

Gordon called Olivia Randle and apologized, suffering the icy voice at the other end of the telephone line. He very much expected to lose her business. A shame, since she was probably taking more medications than anyone else in town. Then, with much trepidation, he broke the news to Cynthia. His heart sank when he saw her face crumple.

"I'll not be going either, then," she said.

Escaping to the third floor, dusty rooms that had once been servant quarters, Cynthia cried through the supper hour and late into the night.

Early the next day she awoke with the exhaustion crying brings. Like a prisoner, she allowed herself to be led to the station wagon. Gwen let her sit in Daisy's usual spot, between the grown-ups in the front seat. Lost was her will to rebel. Instead, she decided to go along and punish them with her misery.

Jane sat at her bedroom window in the chintz-covered chair where she looked out upon the world. It was a perfect day. A sweet breeze with no hint of humidity lifted the sheer curtains. She watched the Craig station wagon as it travelled west out of town toward the city. She was disappointed, yes. But not angry. Jane did not feel things as keenly as Cynthia. She knew Cynthia would suffer over the loss of this day for a long time, tripping over herself to make it up to her. Funny. Jane did not anticipate things with much enthusiasm. She had been disappointed many times.

She imagined telling Cynthia that it was no big deal.

"When we are sixteen, Cyn, I shall have my license and we shall go to the CNE alone. Just the two of us. We can ride the Flyer then. Have patience. It's only four years away." Jane smiled to herself, enjoying the idea of her "generous friend" role. Jane could be whatever anyone wanted her to be. Cynthia needed a best friend and Jane knew how to be that friend.

Poor, cynical Cynthia. Who would she ride the Flyer with today? Near-sighted Lorna, that's who. Cynthia called her the "meanest meanie in Meantown." Only last week, Lorna had lured the girls into the walk-in bank vault in the Craig's cellar and locked them inside. For the better part of an hour she calmed Cynthia in the black prison, which was crawling with real or imagined spiders and centipedes, by telling her ghost stories she had heard at camp.

When Lorna had released them, Jane casually tossed off a remark about how Lorna should take her boyfriends in there.

"They wouldn't be able to see a thing, Lorna. You might get more second dates." Then she ran like hell. Funny how unattractive girls could be so spiteful. Still, Lorna was strangely amusing in a way Jane found intriguing. She was smart and witty and she didn't take any crap from people.

Jane stretched, lifted her cotton nighty over her head and pulled on a fresh blouse. She found herself looking forward to a day without Cynthia's cloying proximity.

At the CNE, Cynthia didn't want to betray Jane by enjoying the day. But the sights and sounds of the Canadian National Exhibition made the maintenance of her despair hard work. And indeed, the Scrambler, the Ferris wheel, and especially the Flyer would have been so much more fun had she shared it with Jane. But Jane was not there and she gradually saw the waste in pouting. Besides, Lorna was in a good mood for once, hooking her arm through Cynthia's and keeping her cruel criticism to a minimum.

It was a memorable family outing. Gwen, without the extra care that Daisy caused her, laughed and took photos with her Brownie camera. It was a busy, lovely day. They stayed at the waterfront until dark to watch the fireworks, then piled into the station wagon for the trip home. The children were all asleep before Gordon turned off Lakeshore Boulevard onto the Queen Elizabeth Way.

Gwen talked quietly to Gordon as he drove through Oakville and Burlington, but she did not confide the idea that had nagged at her all day. That Jane Randle would not have been any trouble. What harm would it have done, Gwen asked herself. What a spoilsport I am. The poor girl must have spent a miserable day alone.

She sent a silent prayer to God to help her be less selfish.

Jane. Lovely Jane. Her red hair bobbed and bouncing, her saddle shoes skipping along the sidewalk toward the stores downtown. Olivia had briefly thought about cancelling her golf game and doing something special with Jane to make up for her disappointment. Then she changed her mind. If anyone had some making up to do, it was the Craigs. She had never liked Gwen, sloppy in scuffed loafers and stained dresses. Instead she decided to leave a five-dollar bill beside Jane's cereal bowl at the kitchen table.

"Treat yourself to something special," Olivia's note suggested.

Jane bought a ball. A red, white and blue rubber ball that cost twenty-five cents at the hardware store. She pocketed the change and went to the empty schoolyard, mindful of the first day of school only a week away.

Jane sang as she bounced the ball over and under her right leg, then her left. She played a game of onesies-twosies against the red brick wall near the girl's entrance. Built in 1903, the cornerstone read. Weeds pushed their way up through the pavement on the playground. She thought of Cynthia clutching the safety bar on the Flyer.

Eventually, Jane headed for home, taking the round about route up Alder Street and across Helena, bouncing the ball ahead of her. It landed in the ditch a few times and she rescued it, wiping the dirt onto her white shorts, knowing it would upset Verna, the housekeeper, but not caring.

Verna would have sandwiches waiting, cut into crustless triangles. She hoped they were not cucumber again. Her mother thought cucumber sandwiches were perfect for summer, but Jane was sick of them. They did not fill her up. She preferred the peanut butter and jam sandwiches that the Craig children made for themselves on great thick slabs of homemade bread.

When she reached the corner of Broad and Helena the factory whistle blew. Jane never failed to feel proud that it was her father's whistle that the town set their clocks by. On an impulse, instead of turning left to go home, she kept on going straight ahead toward the river. She would pay Daddy a visit. Maybe she could talk him into treating her to lunch at the Confectionery downtown.

"Look at all the cars in front of the Randle's place, Gwen," Gordon said.

"Funny that Olivia would have one of her famous soirees on a week night," Gwen replied, rousing from sleep. "It's well after midnight, too."

161

Robert, Jane's big brother was sitting on the curb with his head in his hands. Dr. Warren was sitting beside him with an arm around his shoulders. Gwen's stomach turned over as Gordon slowed the car down and rolled down the window.

"Troubles at your house, Robert?" Gordon asked.

"Janie got hit by a car."

"She died," Dr. Warren added.

"Who died?" Cynthia asked.

Gordon drove the two blocks home through the cricket-noisy night and pulled into their driveway, not daring to look at Gwen or Cynthia.

Lying in bed that night after Dr. Warren had helped him get Cynthia to bed with a strong sedative, Gordon put his arm around his wife.

"You can't blame yourself," he assured her.

"Why would I blame myself?" Gwen asked, staring at the reflection of the street lamp against her bureau.

Cynthia never forgave her mother. Ever. It was not because she blamed her mother for Jane's death. At twelve, Cynthia understood the random cruelty of accidents. It was what she overheard her mother saying to Auntie Kathleen that was unforgivable.

"I'm just glad I didn't take her to the CNE with us," she said. "Imagine how I'd have felt if Jane had been killed in my care. You know I've always believed in fate. When your number's up, well, it's up. Death won't be cheated. Jane's number was up. I knew it would have been a mistake to bring her. My instincts are seldom wrong."

For the rest of her life, Cynthia mourned the loss of her one true friend. If she had stayed home that day, she was sure the accident never would have happened. Or, if her mother was right and the world was governed by fate, perhaps she could have thrown herself under the wheels of the car, saving Jane and becoming a hero.

Everyone accepted blame. Rita Walker never forgave herself for hopping in her car to go to the market. If she had just stayed to answer the phone instead of ignoring it as she walked out the front door, then Jane would have been well away from River Street when she drove by. She would never, ever forget the last look on the little girl's face as she darted out from behind the parked pick-up truck. It was sheer horror.

Olivia admonished herself for not taking the day away from the club. She'd won a bag of tees that day for low net, but lost her daughter.

Verna's heart was broken. She was always uncomfortable when Jane wandered about town on her own. Of course it wasn't her business how the Randles raised their children. Still, she wished she had asked Jane to help her bake some cookies as she sometimes did during the school year.

Despite what she had said to her sisters, Gwen wanted to turn back time and agree to let the little Randle girl join them at the CNE. She couldn't stand herself. She had been responsible for the death of her daughter's best friend and Cynthia did not let her forget it.

Gordon wished he had been more insistent with Gwen about including Jane in the outing. Put his foot down, as it were.

Robert blamed himself for wishing his sister dead. Ironically, the first short story that his English teacher assigned that September was *The Monkey's Paw*. Be careful what you wish for . . .

Everyone accepted blame, except Ralph Randle. He kept his blame to himself. Only Lorie Anderson who had been sitting on his lap, knew what had sent Jane running across River Street without looking both ways. Carelessly, he had forgotten to lock his office door. Up until that day, he had never felt guilty for his flirtations at the factory. He was clever at rationalizing his behaviour, citing a frigid wife as the cause of it. After August 24th 1950 (the date on his daughter's marble headstone) he stayed faithful to Olivia as a penance for his sin. Stayed faithful, that is, until Wendy Johnson came to work for him.

The houses on Broad Street are still standing. Number 400, the Randle place, was inherited by Robert after Olivia's death. Olivia had become somewhat of a recluse after Ralph was found dead of a heart attack in his office, pinning his ninety-pound bookkeeper underneath him. Miss Johnson's screams attracted enough of a crowd that she moved back to Hamilton shortly after. Olivia, who had been blissfully unaware of the nature of Ralph's shift work, gradually faded out of the Lochlin social scene. In the last year of her life, according to the housekeeper, she did not get out of bed, letting Verna feed and toilet her like an infant.

Robert opened a law practice downtown. He had inherited his mother's love of entertaining and, although his parties did not improve his reputation for being a smart aleck, his invitations were sought after by the Lochlin elite. No one could deny that Robert, with his unerring fashion sense, had a flair for good food and fine wine. Oddly, he never married. When people were rude enough to inquire as to the reason why, he claimed he never could find a woman who could take care of him like Verna. He always made sure that Verna was within earshot when he said it. One fall night in the mid-seventies he drove his car into a tree on the way home from the theatre in Toronto and people whispered among each other.

"Remember Jane? It was a car that killed Jane too. Strange. That's the end of the Randle line, then."

Number 334 Broad Street, the Craig's Georgian Manor, opened its doors to dozens of foster children in the years after Jane's death. Gwen was always tired and careworn, but she devoted herself to children in need.

Lorna left town and became a poet and a painter. She play-acted at being a Beatnik and then slipped into the hippy movement, finding refuge in the artist communities of America; San Francisco, Greenwich Village, Soho. Peace, love and feminism suited her, and the drugs improved her self-esteem. Eventually she returned to Canada where she attended The Ontario College of Art and opened a studio in Yorkville.

Gordon's pharmacy continued to be successful until James, his eldest, joined him in business in 1955. Jimmy, as he was still often called no matter how many times he introduced himself as James, did not have his father's meticulous skills, or his discretion. His penchant for gossip after a few draft beers in the Queen's Hotel assured that every teenager on birth control pills was known to the community at large.

Bob Craig married Carolyn Walker (whose mother's car had killed Jane Randle). They both taught at the high school and lived with their two children in a new back-split in the north end.

Cynthia became a registered nurse and worked at the Medical Center. People accepted her nasty personality knowing that she hadn't been quite right since she lost her childhood friend at twelve years of age. Fortunately, her nursing skills were faultless. In her mid-thirties, with the threat of turning into an old maid like her crazy aunts, she married a Bell Telephone lineman when he asked her. He was ten years her senior and set in his ways. Ray was his name. He drank half a dozen beers every night after work, fell asleep on the couch and then woke up around midnight expecting Cynthia to get up and fix him a bite to eat. Doctors and patients alike noted that marriage had made her meaner than ever.

When the Monarch Knitting Factory closed in 1972, the building sat empty for thirty years, haunted by a little red-haired girl. Until the crumbling structure was replaced with riverfront condos, Lochlin school children threw rocks at the broken windows and taunted the ghost with their grandparents' gossip.

Her mother was a snob.

Her fornicating daddy owned the factory.

All the money in the world can't save you if you don't look both ways before you cross the street.

Spoonbills

She didn't plan it.

In the weeks that follow the grey disaster of Christmas, Emma goes to bed early and wakes up at two in the morning. Luckily, Foodland is open around the clock and even though she doesn't need anything, it helps to push a cart up and down the aisles and talk to the checkout woman. Betty is her name. She doesn't sleep either. That's why she took the job.

Since Matthew left, Emma has been a refugee moving from one camp to the next. Crying camp. Self-improvement camp. Meltdown camp. Meditation camp. Emma really didn't expect to find herself single at sixty. Theirs had been a marriage of typical struggles. Matthew did seasonal work as a hunting and fishing guide and, in the winter, he was a ski instructor at the local hill. He had a talent for encouraging adult beginners. Women in particular.

Emma committed herself to a career in health education. She had the big benefits package. Medical, dental, life insurance and a decent pension. A pension that was funding a flat in Ho Chi Minh City for Matthew and his *Little Butterfly*. Forty years of marriage can't compete with daily blowjobs from an attentive Asian woman.

If Matthew had died, Emma would have received half a million in life insurance. Bye-bye line of credit. She invented seven ways to kill him, but in the end she just let him have half of everything. Cars, savings, house, investments. Against the advice of her lawyer and her financial advisor, she stayed in the family home thinking her daughters still needed a little stability in their lives. Now she's broke. She needs new appliances and a new furnace and can't afford them. The real estate woman, divorced and sympathetic, is putting the house on the market in January. Emma has no clue where she'll end up, but she is picturing an apartment downtown with a rusty balcony.

December was bleak. Most days, Emma stayed in her housecoat. There was a deep ache in her muscles that made it hard to carry a load of laundry down to the basement. The ache penetrated to her bones. She was damaged right down to the skeletal level. Pain changes everything, even Christmas. On Christmas morning, she stood at the kitchen sink with her hand up the butt of a twenty-pound turkey and pulled out a paper sack filled with a neck and a liver and a heart and another organ. Maybe a gizzard? She wondered how it is possible that, after preparing forty or fifty turkeys in her lifetime, this is the first time she paused to consider the horror of killing a living creature and stuffing it with it's own body parts. Emma closed her fingers around the hard little heart and vowed that this turkey would be her last. She dressed the bird with apologies and grandmother's special stuffing.

With the potatoes peeled, Emma tidied the bathroom and arranged the gifts she'd purchased for her daughters and their . . . what? Boyfriends? Partners? Her daughters were very different. Lydia was blond and bubbly. Andrea was dark and intense. They never agreed on anything until recently. They agreed that Emma was losing it and probably would end up in the loony bin any day.

Back in the summer, Andrea tried to kidnap Emma's dog, claiming that her mother was no longer capable of caring for Angus. It was true that Emma had neglected the dog a bit since Matthew moved to Ho Chi Minh City. Angus was his dog, after all. A slobbery old spaniel with warts and incontinence. She went to a party in October and drank too much and the host insisted she stay overnight. Angus was in the garage. He was fine, but her nosy neighbor called Andrea and reported that Angus howled half the night. Andrea showed up to rescue Angus but Emma was not prepared to let him go. There was a bit of a scene. The police came. Angus stayed. A house with only one heartbeat is pathetic.

So Christmas dinner was tense. The girls were watching her with the keen observation of research scientists hoping to prove their theories. Here was all the evidence they needed. Emma forgot cranberry sauce. She spelled Andrea's boyfriend's name wrong on his gift. He was Jon. Not John. And she gave Lydia a rice-maker. The same rice-maker that Lydia had given Emma for her birthday last April.

Last April, Emma had been in meltdown camp. Her memory of that particular birthday was hazy. So when she found the rice-maker in her bedroom closet two weeks before Christmas, Emma thought she must have bought it and tucked it away for a gift. Her daughters looked at her like she just stuck a knife in Lydia's gut. What a horrible mother. What a whack job.

The day could not be recovered. Dinner was quick and quiet and everyone declined pumpkin pie in favour of getting back to the city before the snow started. In the early morning hours of Boxing Day, Emma heard ice pellets hit her bedroom window. The storm lasted three days. Sleet. Snow. Wet snow. Emma didn't venture outside except to take seven garbage bags to the curb. All the leftovers from Christmas dinner, all the dollar store gifts, the old-lady sweater with the unmistakable Value Village smell that Lydia had bought her. And Angus, who she found frozen to the back step. She double bagged him and put him in the bin. Out of respect, she tossed the drooping poinsettia (from Jon, not John) on top of the body and said a quick Hail Mary before she put the lid on. God, how she wished she was Catholic. Rosary beads would be a comfort.

Emma stopped eating. She would do the world a favour and starve herself to death. But after two days of that, she ordered a pizza and binge-watched the entire seven seasons of Weeds on Netflix. The next day she ordered Chinese. Then she saw a commercial that informed her that Swiss Chalet delivered. Aside from delivery people, no one called or came by. Her friends were busy with grandchildren and normal things.

Emma's psychiatrist told her she was a cork bobbing on the ocean without purpose, without direction. She had to get herself into a routine. Join a gym. Take a course. Volunteer at a soup kitchen. All those options made Emma want to stick a needle in her eye.

At three in the morning, the Foodland parking lot is empty except for *The Globe and Mail* van. A woman carries a stack of newspapers into the store. Emma used to read the daily paper religiously. After dinner was over and the dishes were done, it was her reward. Now she allows herself to be bombarded by other people's opinions of the news through online sites like *The*

Huffington Post. She and Matthew used to have lively discussions about religion and politics and world events. Emma wonders if he misses conversation. *Little Butterfly*, if her emails are any indication, has limited English skills.

She decides that there is nothing she needs at Foodland and goes to visit her other all-night friend, Andy, at the café. She sits at the table near the window and checks email on her tablet. Nothing friendly, just some come-ons from the whores on 7th Avenue, which is how Emma refers to the pop ups for dating sites.

Andy tries to talk her into chamomile tea, but she insists on an extra large coffee and a bagel with cream cheese. Make it to go, she says. I'm headed out of town.

And that was it. She doesn't even stop at home to grab some underwear and turn the heat down, she just pulls onto the highway and drives west.

Farmers' fields covered in snow stretch endlessly on either side of the 401. Each farm has a light, mounted on a tall pole by the barn. Like lighthouses on a frozen sea, they are reassuring and constant. Emma dated a farmer once, with overalls and a John Deere cap. She could have been a farmer's wife, rising before dawn to tend the animals. There is an alternate Emma out there in the shadow of a silo, her heart listening longingly to the cars whizzing by on the highway.

The sun comes up as she reaches Windsor and Emma follows the signs to the casino. A casino is a good place to get your adrenaline going. It is a good place for people who cannot sleep. It is a good place to feel better about yourself, among so many who are worse off. She plays carelessly, feeding twenties into the slot and pressing the max button repeatedly. Sitting at a Quick Hit machine, Emma decides, is as good a place as any to hit rock bottom.

But instead, she wins eleven thousand dollars.

As she waits for her cashier's cheque, she realizes that her whole body is humming like a machine. There is a buzzing in her chest that feels dangerous. Her skin is too tight.

I-75 takes her due south. Ohio. Kentucky. When she gasses up in Tennessee the temperature is fifty-five degrees Fahrenheit and she starts to cry for the sheer relief of it all. She checks into a Best Western suite in Georgia and sleeps for twenty hours. When she wakes up, she realizes three things. She is going to die someday, but not today. She is a speck in the universe. She can do whatever the hell she wants.

Emma pulls off the interstate in Bradenton, Florida and finds a Wal-Mart. She buys a pair of shorts, a white tee shirt, and some flip flops that have been marked down to ninety-nine cents. After a burger and a shake at Checkers, Emma pulls into the Paradise Cove Carefree RV Resort. There are about three hundred trailers around a pond.

"We call it a lake," Don tells her at the office. "We can rent you a nice little Adventurer for two-fifty." He takes a key off the hook and opens the door of a trailer that smells like microwave popcorn.

"It's just that . . . " Emma said.

"I can go down to two hundred."

"A week?"

"Yep."

"I'll take it."

She signs a paper, gives Don a damage deposit, and heads back to Wal-Mart for some bedding. Two good pillows, a down comforter and some high-end Egyptian cotton sheets. She also buys a padded lawn chair, a book, and four bottles of wine.

Sitting in the sun between the Adventurer and the lake, Emma checks her phone. *Where's Angus?* is all Lydia wants to know.

Angus and I took a little trip to paradise. Maybe you could drop by the house and turn the heat down. She takes a picture of two wading birds and attaches it to the text message.

The birds step delicately through the weeds at the edge of the lake. Pink, like flamingos, but with wide beaks, like spatulas. She does a quick search and finds that they are called Spoonbills. These birds are monogamous, Wikipedia tells her, but only for a year at a time.

"Pretty, huh? This is a real migration path. Lots of different birds pass through. Some of 'em stick around for awhile and some of 'em take off elsewhere."

Emma turns to see a woman wearing a turquoise bathing suit. Despite bulges of unsightly flesh, she is totally at ease in her skimpy swimwear.

"I'm Leona."

"Emma."

"Welcome to Horseshoe Cove. You might want to move your chair out into the shade a bit. You could use a little colour, but you got to take it easy."

"Thanks," Emma says.

"Happy Hour's at four on the clubhouse patio," Leona tells her. "Drinks are two bucks each. I'll come by and get you."

Emma watches as Leona retreats to a double-wide with a screened porch. Later, she will learn it is called a lanai, not a porch. She will learn the language and fit in. She will take up shuffleboard and step-dancing and canasta. She will meet a retired professor who will take her bird watching in the Everglades. She will practice monogamy for a year, or as long as it suits her.

Corn Roast

Fran McCann pushed her husband's wheelchair over the hard, rutted clay toward the bonfire where five men stood around watching Jeff Lymburner dump a wheelbarrow load of split logs onto a pile beside the shed. The fire would last all night.

Rick bounced along, uncomplaining, though Fran knew the jostling was aggravating the sores he had developed on his lower back. He held a small cooler in his lap with everything he needed for the party, rye and coke and ice and a plastic mug with a Toronto Maple Leafs logo on it. It matched his cap, the peak pulled low over his eyes shading them from the setting September sun.

If she hadn't heard all their stories before, Fran might have assumed, by the raucous laughter, that they were sharing a funny anecdote. But the hyped up hilarity was most likely for Rick's benefit. A year and a half ago, Ricky could have wrestled any one of them to the ground. He could out-skate them all. The new Ricky would never lace up again and the loud back slapping congeniality was their way of offering an awkward apology.

"I'm going to leave you with this bunch, sweetie," Fran told him when they got close enough so the men could hear. "I'll go and help Linda with the salads."

"Ricky-boy," Arnie Waters yelled. "Let's get you a drink, my man. You got some catching up to do."

"You might want to shuck some of that corn before you all get loaded," Fran suggested as she kicked the wheelchair brake into place.

"Yes, dear," Rick said in a squeaky falsetto. The men howled.

Fran stepped around the rotting boards as she climbed the back steps and entered the farmhouse kitchen. Linda Lymburner was wiping the counter. She had an apron tied over jeans and a tee shirt. Linda was the only one of Fran's friends who wore an apron in the kitchen. It made her look old-fashioned, even though she was only twenty-one. Just three years ago she'd been a cheerleader for the football heroes out at the fire and now she was their mother hen.

"What can I do?" Fran asked.

"Fran. Thank god you're here. I got three dozen hard boiled eggs in the fridge need peeling."

Linda treated Fran the same as ever. She had been her maid of honour. They had talked on the phone every day since grade ten and they kept it up after they got married six weeks apart, summer before last. When Ricky had his accident, Linda called every day. She'd get Fran laughing over some dumb-ass thing that happened at work or talk about the boots on sale in the Sears catalogue. Did Fran think she should get the black leather or the brown suede?

"And by the way, there is a guy works for my dad that can outfit your house for wheelchair access. Don't worry about the cost, neither. Me and Rosemarie are getting a fundraiser going."

Linda's voice gave Fran the courage to take a look at her new reality with confidence.

I can handle this. "You want these eggs devilled?" Fran asked.

"Yep. You know how Jeff loves his devilled eggs, even though, lord knows he'll be farting under the covers all night. The platter's under the counter below the kettle there. That's it. The one with the turkey on it." Linda draped Saran Wrap over a big bowl of coleslaw and put it in the fridge. Then she freshened up her rye and coke and sat down at the kitchen table.

"You working tomorrow?" Fran asked. Linda was a part-time cashier at the IGA and Fran was a secretary at the insurance company. They took coffee breaks together at the Kozy Korner.

"No, thank god. I told Mary I was having this corn roast and she offered to put one of the young girls on. She's pretty good about that if you ask her in advance and not the day before. What about you?"

"Housework. Laundry. Hey, are you finished with that new mystery?"

"Ya, you want it?" Linda hopped up and reached on top of the fridge for the paperback.

Fran threw a glop of mayo into the chopped egg yolks. Linda opened the cupboard and grabbed a bottle of paprika from the spice rack. "Let me finish them eggs. Go ahead and put the book in your van so you won't forget it later."

"Thanks, Linda. I'll go out to the fire and check on Rick."

It was fresh outside. Summer was about over. In the twilight the leaves on the beech trees glowed yellow against the shadowy maples. The sumacs were bright red at the end of the lane. It made Fran think about buying some wool so she could start an afghan. She loved having a knitting project as the days got shorter, the wool pooling in her lap as she watched television. Rick was in charge of the clicker, preferring reality shows to sitcoms and sports to drama. She didn't care. Really, she didn't.

Fran unlocked the van and tucked her book between the front seats. The Rotary Club purchased this vehicle for them after Ricky's accident, with a hydraulic lift for the chair and everything. She loved driving it, high up from the road like a truck. And she got the best parking spaces in town.

The crickets were screaming from the ditch alongside the lane as Fran headed toward the fire. Lanny Atkinson had driven his Dodge Charger up to the shed so he could blast his sound system; CCR with too much bass. "Old black water, keep on rollin' . . . Mississippi moon, won't you keep on shinin' on me."

She walked up behind Rick, pulled off his cap and kissed him on the top of his head. He had a full head of dark wavy hair.

"Hey babe."

"Hey Franny."

"What did I miss?"

"Al pulled down his riggin' and showed off his football tattoo. Ron says it looks like a dog turd."

"I would've thought it was a bit early in the evening for that display."

"He's already wasted. Called in sick today. Him and Arnie started drinking at noon."

Fran looked over at Arnie. She had dated him in high school for three years but they broke up in the middle of grade twelve when he went south of the border to play hockey. She cried for five days straight until her mother threatened to book her into the hospital. Arnie looked up and caught her eye. He nodded. She smiled.

"Want a drink, Franny?" Rick asked.

"Sure," she said.

Fran mixed a drink and sat on the cooler beside her husband, enjoying the heat of the fire on her face while a cool autumn wind lifted the curls off the back of her neck. She reached over and took the cigarette out of Rick's hand and dragged on it. Fran hardly smoked anymore, so it gave her a buzz. She listened to conversations rising and falling, the same old bullshit. Not enough ice time at the arena. Moose hunting restrictions. Then she latched onto Rick's conversation with Lloyd Grey, an older guy who owned the car dealership downtown. Jeff's boss.

"You should run for office, Rick. You got a good head on your shoulders. Council needs some young blood, that's for sure. You run in Ward 4 where your parents live, I know you'd get in. Beat out that ornery old Dutchman."

"I don't know, Lloyd. The Dutch Reformed Church is up there on the Second Line. They're a pretty loyal bunch."

"Run anyway. Throw your hat in the ring and people will get the idea you're interested. Then start coming to meetings. Get to know the issues. You'd get a lot of votes from this young crowd, Rick. They respect you. I noticed how they were listening when you were talking about the new housing development."

Lloyd had a few drinks in him, but Fran could tell he was sincere. She felt good that Lloyd took Rick seriously. He was smart, her husband. An Ontario Scholar in grade twelve. Now he was taking some university courses through correspondence. Business. Fran squeezed Rick's hand and got up, lifted the top of the cooler and mixed another drink for herself, then took Rick's glass and mixed him up a strong one. She didn't want him drinking too much Coke. If Lloyd hadn't been sitting so close, she would've checked Rick's bag to see how full it was getting. It made her realize she needed to take a pee herself.

Fran started walking away from the fire toward the house, then remembered the outhouse behind the barn. She turned and stepped through Linda's vegetable garden, the drying tomato stalks brushing against her jeans. Her boots made a sucking sound in the soft soil. She heard the outhouse door close and latch as she approached, so she crouched in the shadows and waited. Within a minute, four grey kittens were mewing around her feet. She picked up the littlest one but put it down fast when she saw the pus oozing out the eye. Barn cats. Yuck. The latch clicked on the outhouse door.

"Hey, Franny," Arnie said, zipping his fly.

"I hear you got an early start today," Fran said.

"What?"

"Drinking. Rick said you and Al started early."

"Yeah."

"Are the rumors true that you're headed to Sweden soon? To play hockey?"

"Norway. Yeah, I leave at the end of next week."

Fran knew better than anyone how bad Arnie had wanted to get drafted by the NHL. Of all the guys on the Juvenile team, he had the best chance of making it to the big show. He could play, but he could also think. And he was a leader. Captain every year. He knew how to encourage the other guys. How to set a high standard for sportsmanship.

He went to Pennsylvania and played for the Erie Otters when he was nineteen but he broke his collarbone twice that season and the scouts passed him by. Still, the European teams paid well, and there wasn't the same risk of getting hurt over there. They play a faster game, not so much checking.

"Well, good luck."

Arnie was standing close enough that she could smell his leather jacket. She had an urge to press herself into that familiar curve of chest and stomach. Her head would rest against the pocket of his flannel shirt. It would smell of Ivory Snow. They had loved each other with the uncomplicated affection of grade school sweethearts. Valentines and bike rides and hours on the phone. She sat behind the bench and watched him play Pee Wee, Bantam, Midget. He practiced her lines with her and attended every performance when she played Desdemona, Linda Loman, Maria.

"Thanks, Franny," he said, turning. "Take care of yourself." He paused, then started walking away. Fran's heart dropped into her stomach as she watched his silhouette against the glow of the fire. She stepped up into the outhouse but left the door open. If anyone was coming, she'd see them in plenty of time.

When she got back to the fire, the water in the big iron pot was boiling. Jeff was throwing in the first couple dozen cobs of corn. Linda was setting out butter and salt and paper towels on the picnic table.

"Buns and cold-cuts and salads inside whenever anyone's hungry," she called.

"I'll go in and fix Ricky a plate before he gets too hammered," she told Linda. But when she stopped to ask Rick what he wanted, she ended up having a drink. And another. Then she got them both some corn.

"Okay, I'm going to get you a plate," she said. "And I mean it this time."

"Gimme loss of Linda's poe-dae-do salad," Rick slurred.

Fran stepped out of the warmth of the fire into the frontier of country darkness. She stepped high to avoid tripping and cautiously carried her hands in front of her until her eyes adjusted to the night. Arnie must have been watching her because he stood up too. She saw him out the corner of her eye and she walked, not to the house as she had intended, but back alongside the corn cribs. Arnie was right beside her and she fell into him and she was sixteen again. She let him lead her out into the cornfield without exchanging so much as one word. He remembered her body and she remembered his.

Even on the night they broke up, they had fit together effortlessly. Dancing the last slow dance in the high school gym, the decorations hanging in ruins from the basketball nets, the air humid with hormones, they clung together like there was a war going on and this was the last chance for a little comfort.

But Arnie's dad convinced him that he should *play the field*. That having only one high school girlfriend was limiting his opportunities. He was athlete of the year, for crying out loud. He deserved to have a little fun.

Linda watched the big dipper over Arnie's shoulder. She thought he had fallen asleep, his breathing was deep and even. The corncob that she was lying on was starting to hurt, digging into her ribs and sure to give a bruise. She tried to move and Arnie rolled away from her. She laughed. Gave him the cob.

"Pig corn," he said. "Not good for eating."

"Always the smooth talker," Fran said.

"I'll go back first," Arnie said, pushing himself up and zipping his leather jacket as he walked toward the light.

Fran sat up and hugged her knees to her chest. She listened to the sound of a dog barking over on the next farm and allowed herself to feel a little bit sorry that she was Fran McCann instead of Fran Waters. She knew in her heart that if Arnie showed up

on her doorstep next week and asked her to go to Norway with
him she probably would.

At the fire, Rick was asleep in his chair. Passed out cold,
with his mouth open and his head tilted at an awkward angle.
His plastic Leafs cup lay on the ground beside the empty Crown
Royal bottle. He was the only one left at the fire except for Lanny
who was passed out on the front seat of his car, his legs dangling
out the passenger door. Fran knelt beside the wheelchair and
pulled Rick's sweat pants down. His bag was full. She pinched
the catheter and pulled the bag off and emptied the urine into
the grass. Then she reattached the bag and pulled up her husband's pants and rinsed her hands off in the melted ice inside
the cooler. She stood up and threw an empty Coke carton into
the fire, watching while it flared up like a Beltane ceremony.
Fertility, she prayed while the sparks crackled. Then she wheeled
Rick back to the van.

Inside, the kitchen was too bright. The florescent light over
the sink made Linda look sickly. Fran popped a devilled egg
into her mouth and said goodnight.

"I'm on my way, Linda. Ricky's out in the van, already asleep.
Thanks. It was a fun night."

"You want your lasagna pan?"

"Is it empty?"

They walked into the dining room and saw the pan was still
about a third full.

"I'll come by tomorrow or Sunday and pick it up."

"You sure?"

Fran noticed Arnie, sitting on an ottoman in the living room
with a plate on his lap. He had a bun halfway to his mouth. He
lifted his eyebrows at her. She smiled.

"Yeah. Thanks for the book. You want it back or should I pass it on to Carol?"

"Pass it on. It's no prize winner."

Fran zipped up her jacket and turned to go.

"Wait," Linda said. "You got something on your back." Linda pulled a long yellow leaf off Fran's jacket. "Corn husk," she said. She could have thrown it in the garbage, but no. She handed it to Fran like it was a strand of crepe paper from the senior prom. Her eyes said, *Tuck that away in your memory box now and carry on. You're all right. Everything's going to be all right.*

Funny how it never turns out like you think. Rick hitting his head on the bottom of the pool in Disney World on their honeymoon. Fran, always envied in high school for her camp counselor good looks and the easy way she had of talking to people, thought that no one would envy her ever again. But they did. Her and Rick bought the prettiest house up on Skyline Drive. She took over her Dad's insurance business. Rick sat on town council for twelve years and then ran for mayor. Won against the incumbent by a landslide. They went to Florida every winter for three weeks. Never had kids, though. So.

Arnie stayed on in Norway and got married to a fashion model who appeared in *Vogue* magazine once or twice. Fran thought she looked kind of mean. Something about her eyes. Just last year Arnie came home, divorced and dying of testicular cancer. His mother met Fran out front of the Kozy not too long after the funeral and asked her to drop by.

"Arnie had something he wanted me to give you," she said.

Fran popped in a few days later. The house hadn't changed much since the times she had come over as a teenager, as

Arnie's girlfriend. She remembered the tea kettle wallpaper in the kitchen. Mrs. Waters opened a drawer and pulled out a dried-out cob of corn.

"He said to me, he said give this to Franny and tell her she was the love of my life."

He knew, didn't he, that she would have packed her bags and gone with him. All he had to do was say the word and she'd have left her husband. Left her friends. Left the town she grew up in. But it wasn't the right thing to do.

Mrs. Waters pulled her in tight for a hug and Fran breathed in the smell of Ivory Snow.